Laundromat
Blues

Laundromat Blues

Stories by

Lupe Solis, Jr.

Minnesota Voices Project Number 82

NEW RIVERS PRESS 1997

Copyright © 1997 by Lupe Solis, Jr.
Library of Congress Catalog Number 97-65064
ISBN 0-89823-177-9
All rights reserved
Edited by Debra Marquart
Book design and typesetting by Barb Patrie Graphic Design
Cover illustration by Jansson Stegner

New Rivers Press is a nonprofit literary press dedicated to
publishing the very best emerging writers in our region, nation,
and world.

The publication of *Laundromat Blues: Stories by Lupe Solis, Jr.*
has been made possible by generous grants from the Jerome
Foundation, the Metropolitan Regional Arts Council (from an
appropriation by the Minnesota Legislature), the North Dakota
Council on the Arts, the South Dakota Arts Council, Target
Stores, Dayton's and Mervyn's by the Dayton Hudson
Foundation, and the James R. Thorpe Foundation.

Additional support has been provided by the Elmer L. and
Eleanor J. Andersen Foundation, the Beim Foundation, General
Mills Foundation, Liberty State Bank, the McKnight
Foundation, the Minnesota State Arts Board (through an
appropriation by the Minnesota Legislature), the Star
Tribune/Cowles Media Company, the Tennant Company
Foundation, and the contributing members of New Rivers Press.
New Rivers is a member agency of United Arts.

Laundromat Blues: Stories by Lupe Solis, Jr. has been manufac-
tured in the United States of America for New Rivers Press,
420 North 5th Street, Suite 910, Minneapolis, MN 55401.
First Edition.

For family:

*The Solis's, Gonzales's, Kosioreks, Gutierrez's, Samudios,
Zellmers, Zimmers, Heimans, Jacobos, Bodellos, Rangles, and
Leons. For the ones who passed on the legacies for our future,
this book is dedicated to our living history. . . .*

Acknowledgments

Special thanks to New Rivers Press's Minnesota Voices Project for creating an outlet for new writers. I would like to thank the Word Warriors writing group at the University of Wisconsin–Milwaukee for the years of love and support of my work. And, special thanks to the Creative Writing Department at UW–Milwaukee for the opportunity to study with some of the best writers in the country. Warm thanks to my family and friends for their support.

Special acknowledgments go to the editors of the publications that published my first few short stories: *The Cream City Review*: "Laundromat Blues"; *Hayden's Ferry Review*: "The Secret"; *Blue Dawn, Red Earth: New Native American Storytellers* (Anchor Books): "El Sol."

The quotations in "Mousetrap" are from Gerald Vizenor's *Interior Landscapes* and are used with permission of the author.

The quotation in "To Say Goodbye" from *Love in the Time of Cholera* by Gabriel Garcia Marquez is used with permission of Random House, Inc.

Table of Contents

Preface

I offer up these stories as a celebration of influence from the people, places, and things that have made up my world. My stories spring from the place where I was born, and my extended family that connected, and still connects, me to the larger world. In here there are names and places that resonate some of my beginnings, travails, sadnesses, and triumphs. But what must be said is in all fiction—the truth lies in the telling of a story, not words or things taken out of the "real" world. This book is therefore a celebration of familial ties from here to Mexico to Poland.

I have lately come to know small bits of my Mestizo heritage. Unlike my Polish heritage, from which most of my story-telling ability springs, the "other" half was only whispered in ashamed asides. "We are American," I was told when I asked. Not "Mexican," "Indian," "Mestizo" (that dirty half-breed word), God forbid "Chicano." We played the game of acceptance in a world that demanded categories to remind us of our differences.

In recognition of history lost, I offer up a Spanish translation of my first story, *"El Sol,"* which has its place in my heart that yearns for a language almost alien to the main character and myself.

Peace.

Lupe Solis, Jr.

I.
To Say Good-bye

Hear Your Voice

I knew you well, so long ago.
If I could tell you what you should know
that my heart is breaking up inside
and my love for you may never die.

If I could hold you just one more time,
I know you would feel the same as I
that your heart is tearin' up inside
and your love for me would never die.

Then I hear your voice again
after all this time gone by.
Then I hear your voice again
and it makes me wonder why
this time, I just can't say good-bye. . . .

"Hear Your Voice,"
music and lyrics by Jim Gutierrez and Jose Berrios

Soul Chant

chant alma

chant
sol

shine

sunshine
brightens every room
running through the fields
running through the woods

soul   sol
              sol
shine   brightens
           brightens

tía gama
ama sol

running through the fields
running through the woods

```
sol        alma
       tía
brightens     gama


village         sol-
       is on e fire d up
brightens
       is
       one
       fine

high step
soul step       is
       one
       fine
sol        soul
```

Peter Whalen

El Sol

Lying next to the tree with his eyes closed, he imagined himself blind. The warm fingers of the sun danced across his hairless legs and chest, touching his face in tentative caresses. He listened to the rustle of tall grass and the rhythms of his heartbeat. His hands squeezed the moist earth, trying to see the greenness with his skin; the leaves above him chattered in the stronger gusts of wind. In the distance he heard the rumble of a train, probably dropping boxcars off at the paper mill.

The late August rays felt good on his almost naked body; in his well-worn sneakers, cutoffs, and T-shirt lying next to him—he felt like a castaway. He tried to feel the world, as his tía had asked him to do. She was in the final stages of her leukemia. At twelve he knew some things and some things he didn't understand, but he was sure that his tía was dying.

He tried to open himself fully to the world around him, the whoosh of cars from the distant street, the smell of the grass, the audible thump of birds beating their wings against the wind.

His body was starting to itch, defeating his senses. Sighing, he sat up and brushed the grass from his arms and back, feeling the indents left on his skin—a reminder that he was only a visitor here and not a resident. He stood, threading his T-shirt into a belt loop. It struck him again as he looked at the distant street, how two different worlds could exist so close together. He lived a block away in a place of people, houses, and cars. Here, he felt small. Once he crossed the railroad tracks, he was alone with the fields and the sky.

He turned his back on the houses and ran into the wild. His legs never tired: he ran and ran and ran. In some places the grass was taller than he was. The trail he followed had been worn down by others seeking escape, too. At times, he dashed into the towering grass, leaping higher and higher as his strides grew stronger. The clouds above paced him, racing him to the lake.

He let himself quietly into the room he shared with his tía, careful not to disturb her in case she was sleeping. She was awake most nights now, in pain, and any kind of rest was welcomed and respected by the family. He looked at the bunk beds he shared with her, the bottom bed was empty except for a rosary hanging above her pillow. His tía was sitting in a rocking chair by the open window.

"Tía," he whispered to the back of the rocker.

"Daemy," her voice rasped, "Come here, I'm not sleeping."

He went to her, grass-stained and dusty.

"You have a good run, Daemy?"

"Yes."

"Rolling in the grass, too?" She inhaled with a wispy smile.

"Yes."

"How is the sky . . . when you ran? Did it follow you?" Her hand waved the air in front of her, a summoning of him and his day.

"Yes," he said again. He knelt by her feet resting his head on her knee, completing their morning ritual.

"The ducklings at the marsh are getting big," he said into her skirt.

"Of course. Soon autumn will be, then they will fly." Her hand lightly touched the back of his head, he could feel the heat of her sickness. "I smell the grass . . . and the marsh, of course, but something else, too . . . " she whispered, then coughed. Gaining control of her voice, she sighed, "Tell me, Daemy."

He told her all about his morning: how his legs seemed to stretch forever when he ran, the marsh grass bending before him, the birds fighting the wind, and how the train's engine growled in his chest. Staring sightlessly out the window, she asked him to repeat parts in more detail, drawing from him pictures of his day.

Every morning he was her eyes, ears, fingers, nose; every morning he pulled out a piece of himself to share with his tía. She had been with his family for two months. His tío, her husband, had run out on her and she had nowhere else to go. His dad had brought her home to live with his family in their small house. "Dameon," his dad had said, "Your tía is *enferma—muy, muy.* She must stay in your room . . . with you."

At first, he was upset at the thought of someone sharing his room, but once she was there, he began to understand. Then, a month ago, she went blind because of her sickness. She didn't complain. Even at night, she tried to muffle her pain so as not to disturb his sleep. Before bed, she would pray to God thanking Him for another day.

Once, he had asked her why she prayed. He wondered why the more she prayed, the sicker she became. Didn't God hear her? And if He did, why was she so sick? She told him that God was helping her with her faith. "What is faith?" he asked her. She didn't answer, but asked him, "When you play tomorrow, will you do something for me?"

"Yes."

"Will you remember everything you see and tell me about it?"

"Okay, . . . I'll try," he answered her, confused.

"Good, Daemy, that's all we can do."

Since then, every morning, he had a mission to *try*. He neglected his friends and began to discover the world beyond the tracks. Every day he changed for her.

The second week in September, he was up late one night listening to her labored breathing, her quiet pain. He shut his eyes tight and prayed to God to help her. Feeling nothing, he rolled to his side using his awakened senses to share in her suffering. When he finally fell asleep, he was drained of all his energy. He slept later than usual and was awakened by his tía's soft crying. His mother was by her side. "Mama . . . ?" he started.

"Shh . . . Your tía has lost her hearing," his mother whispered, as if she needed to.

From then on she sat in her rocker by the window, humming to herself, smiling. He wondered if he should keep up his morning runs for her. Out of habit, he left that morning and ran down the street and over the tracks.

He lost himself.

He came back later and knelt by her chair as before, resting his head on her knee.

"Daemy," she whispered, "How was your run? I can smell the grass and your sweat; you ran hard." Her hand touched his face, his lips. "Speak, Daemy. I can't hear you, but I can feel."

So he spoke as before. He told her about his hard run. Her hand moved gently back and forth across his face and lips. She rocked slowly, smiling as if she saw and heard. Her nostrils expanded, inhaling his day. He didn't know if she understood him, but she was happy. He continued his morning runs.

One morning before he left, his father stopped him. "Dameon, it won't be long now." Dameon sprinted out the front door and headed for the tracks. He stretched his legs out and reveled in the wind and smells of life. As he ran he wondered if in some way God was telling his tía things. The

look on her face was at times happy, yet sad. His legs pound-
ed the ground harder.

Now as he came to her, he brought her things. Once, a
pussy willow. She ran her hands up and down the stalk,
touching the soft, downy top. After a while she smiled,
"Pussy willow." He nodded his head against her knee.
Sometimes he brought rocks—the kind you skip across the
water. Other times he offered flowers, a milk pod, and once,
even a grasshopper. Each day he found something different
to offer. She would sit for hours, smelling and feeling every
gift he presented to her.

When he was out in his new world, he'd sit and pretend he was blind and deaf. Closing his eyes tight, he would
force air into his eardrums, shutting out every sound except
his breathing and heartbeat. In front of him, laid out on the
ground, he would have the things he was bringing for his tía.
He'd grasp an object and try to see with his fingers what he
was holding. Or, hold it to his nose to identify it with smell.

He came home one afternoon to find a note saying his
mother and father had taken his tía to the hospital. It said
he should stay home until they came back.

He went into the bathroom, stripped off his dirty T-
shirt and cutoffs, and climbed into the bathtub. He lay there
soaking, trying to imagine what else God could take away
from her. Lying there with eyes closed, a soft familiar voice
in his heart asked him to run one last time. Run hard and
fast—for me.

He dug his dirty clothes out of the hamper, not even
bothering to dry himself, and put them back on. Forsaking
even his sneakers, he burst out the front door and headed for
the tracks with his wet hair sticking to his forehead. He ran
along the tracks, stretching his legs farther than ever.

The sky was an icy blue and the wind held a breath of
autumn. He turned to the tall grass, and the lake beyond,
breaking stride only to leap the tracks.

He picked up speed.

He thought if he could jump high enough, he could break through and grasp sky. For the first time, he could see over the tall grass. As he leapt higher and higher his legs loosened, and he fixed his eyes on the sun. Fire burned in streaks across his face and pooled into his ears.

He raised his arms and caught the wind.

His feet left the ground.

He was free.

El Sol

Translated by Stellia Jordán Orozco

Tirado junto al árbol con los ojos cerrados, se imaginó ciego. Los dedos tibios del sol bailaban sobre su pecho y piernas lampiñas, acariciándole el rostro, a duras penas tocándolo. Escuchaba el murmurar del pasto y el ritmo de su corazón. Sus manos exprimían la tierra húmeda tratando de sentir el verdor con su piel. Las hojas, encima, chachareaban en las ráfagas de viento. En la distancia se escuchaba el gruñir del tren, quizá dejando los vagones en la fábrica de papel.

Los últimos rayos de agosto le hacían sentir bien; el cuerpo semi desnudo, los tenis viejos, las bermudas, y la camiseta junto a él le hacía sentir como un paria. Quería palpar el mundo como se lo habia pedido su tía. Estaba ya en las últimas etapas de la leucemia. A los doce años sabía muchas cosas, pero muchas otras apenas sí las comprendía; sin embargo, no le cabía la menor duda de que Tía estaba muriendo.

Quería abrirse, completamente, al mundo que le rodeaba: al exhalar de los autos, al olor del prado, al aletear de los pájaros en contra del viento.

Una piquiña empezó a invadirle el cuerpo, venciéndolo. Suspiró, se sentó y se quitó el pasto de su espalda horadada y de sus brazos marcados—recordándole que era sólo transeúnte, no residente. Se paro, y anudo la camiseta en la presilla del pantalón. Al mirar la calle lejana, le sorprendió, de nuevo, que existieran dos mundos tan cercanos, y aún tan distintos. Vivía a una cuadra de la muchedumbre, de las casas y de los carros. Aquí, se sentía insignificante. Al cruzar la carrilera se encontró solo entre el campo abierto y el horizonte.

Le dio la espalda al mundo de la gente y se internó en el indómito. Las piernas nunca se le cansaban: corrió y corrió y corrió. En algunos lugares se perdía entre la altura verde, pero aparecía luego, caminando el sendero ya marcado por el andar de muchos otros. Algunas veces se lanzaba al verdor, disolviéndose en él, materializándose intermitentemente en el ímpetu de sus saltos. Las nubes mantenían su paso, compitiendo con él hasta el lago.

Tratando de no hacer ruido, entró, con cuidado, al cuarto de su tía. No quería despertarla en caso de que durmiera. Se pasaba las noches en vela, con dolor, y cualquier momento de paz era bienvenido y apreciado por la familia. Miró los camarotes. El de abajo estaba vacío excepto por el rosario que colgaba directamente sobre la almohada. Tía estaba sentada en la mecedora junto a la ventana abierta. "Tía," le susurró.

"Daemy," dijo con voz áspera, "Ven aquí, no estoy durmiendo."

Se le acercó, enverdecido y polvoriento.

"¿Te divertiste corriendo, Daemy?"

"Sí."

"¿Y rodaste en la hierba, también?" Inhaló. Sonrisa fina.

"Sí."

"¿Como está el cielo . . . cuando corriste? ¿Te siguió?" Su mano echó a un lado el aire que se interponía, evocando el día y a su sobrino.

"Sí," respondió de nuevo. Se arrodilló a los pies de su

tía, reposando la cabeza en sus rodillas, concluyendo así el ritual matutino.

"Los patitos en la ciénaga están creciendo," dijo él, sus palabras perdiéndose entre los pliegues de la falda.

"¡Por supuesto! Pronto llegará el otoño, y luego, ¡volarán!" Su mano, gentilmente, le tocó la cabeza; el sintió la pasión de su fervor. "Huelo la hierba . . . y el pantano, claro, pero algo más . . . también . . . ," susurró, luego tocó. Recobrando el control de su voz, suspiró, "Cuéntame, Daemy, cuéntame."

Le contó su mañana: como sus piernas parecían estirarse eternamente hasta el infinito cuando corría, la hierba del pantano doblegandose ante él, los pájaros peleando en contra del viento, y como sentía el gruñir de la locomotora en su pecho. Mirando por la ventana con ojos de ciega, le pidió que repitiera ciertas partes en más detalle, trazando así su día con dibujos.

Cada mañana, él era su vista, su oír, su tacto, su olfato; cada mañana arrancaba un pedacito de sí mismo para compartir con su tía. Había estado con ellos desde hacía dos meses. Su esposo la había dejado y no tenía adonde ir. Su padre la había traído a la pequeña casa para que viviera con ellos. "Dameon," le había dicho su padre, "Tu tía está enferma—muy, muy enferma. Debe de quedarse en tú cuarto . . . contigo."

Al principio se molestaba con tan sólo pensar que alguien compartiría su habitación, pero cuando ella llegó, empezó a comprender. Después, hace un mes, perdió la vista. No se quejó. Aun, por la noche, trataba de sofocar el dolor para no turbar el sueño de su sobrino. Antes de acostarse, le rezaba a Dios, y agradecía que le hubiera dado otro día.

Una vez le había preguntado por qué rezaba. No entendía por qué entre más rezaba, más se enfermaba. ¿Acaso Dios no la escuchaba? Y sí lo hacía, ¿por qué

entonces estaba tan enferma? Un dia le había dicho que Dios
la ayudaba con su fe. "¿Qué es la fe?" Ella no contestó, pero
le preguntó, "¿Cuando salgas al campo mañana, harás algo
por mí?"

"Sí."

"¿Recordarás todo lo que veas y me lo contarás?"

"Okay . . . trataré," contestó confundido.

"Bueno, Daemy. Es todo lo que podemos hacer."

Desde entonces, cada mañana, tenía una misión que
cumplir. Abandonó a sus amigos y empezó a descubrir el
mundo mas allá de la carrilera. Cambiaba, cada día, para ella.

Una noche, durante la segunda semana de septiembre,
se quedó despierto hasta muy tarde escuchando el dolor
mudo de su tía, su respiración forzada. Empuñó sus ojos, y le
rogó a Dios que la ayudara. Sin sentir nada, se volteó, y en
un estado de sopor, compartió su sufrimiento. Por fin, agota-
do su energía concilió el sueño. Durmió más de lo usual. El
llanto queto de su tía lo despertó. Al lado, su madre.

"¿Mamá . . . ?"

"Shh . . . ," dijo en voz muy baja, como sí fuera nece-
sario. "Tu tía ya no puede oír."

De ahí en adelante, empezó a sentarse en la mecedora,
junto a la ventana, sonriendo. Él se preguntaba si debía
seguir corriendo para ella. Mecánicamente, a fuerza de cos-
tumbre, salió esa mañana, calle abajo, pasando luego la carrilera.

Se perdió en sí mismo.

Más tarde regresó y se arrodilló junto a la mecedora
como lo había hecho antes, su cabeza, reposando en la rodilla.

"Daemy," susurró, "¿Cómo te fue? Puedo oler el prado y
tu sudor; corriste con gana." Con la mano palpó su cara, tocó
sus labios. "Háblame, Daemy. No puedo oír, pero te puedo
sentir."

Entonces, empezó a contarle todo, como lo había
hecho antes y ella, suavemente, acariciándole el rostro, deja-

ba que las manos, repetidamente, viajaran por su cara, hasta la boca, retornando a la cara, regresando a la boca. Se mecía lentamente, como sí hubiera visto, como si hubiera escuchado. Las ventanas de su nariz se abrían, inhalando el día. No estaba seguro si ella entendía, pero estaba contenta. Continuó corriendo.

Una mañana, antes de salir, su padre lo detuvo. "Dameon, falta poco." Dameon salió a toda velocidad por la puerta del frente y se dirigió a los rieles. Extendiendo las piernas, deleitándose en el viento y en los olores de la vida, se preguntaba, a medida que corría, sí Dios le estaba diciendo cosas a su tía. A veces, aunque triste, parecía contenta. Sus pies parecían golpear la tierra.

Ahora, cuando iba a ella, le traía cosas. Una vez, una rama de sauce. Ella, con suavidad, exploró el tallo en toda su longitud, tocando la cima aterciopelada. Después de un rato, sonrió. "Sauce común." Asintió, su cabeza en sus rodillas. Algunas veces traía piedras—de aquéllas que rebotan sobre el agua al tirarlas. Otras veces le ofrecía flores, las del sauce de hoja sedosa, y aun, un día, un saltamontes. Cada día le traía algo diferente. Se sentaba, por horas y horas, oliendo y tocando cada obsequio.

A veces, en aquel mundo, pretendía ser sordo y mudo. Cerrando los ojos con fuerza, hacía que el aire entrara en sus tímpanos, excluyendo cualquier otro sonido, excepto el de los pulmones y el corazón. En frente de él, los obsequios. Al asirlos, trataba de verlos con los dedos, de indentificarlos al olerlos.

Una tarde, al llegar a casa, encontró una nota de sus padres: que habían llevado a Tía al hospital, que se quedara en casa hasta que regresaran.

Fue al cuarto, se quitó la camiseta sucia y las bermudas, y se metió en la tina. Trató de imaginar qué más podría Dios arrebatarle a Tía. Allí, con los ojos cerrados, una voz familiar le pidió que corriera, una última vez. Corre fuerte y rápido—por mí.

Sacó la ropa sucia de la canasta, y sin secarse, se la puso. Dejando los tenis atrás, irrumpió por la puerta del frente y se dirigió a la carrilera. Corrió, estirando las piernas como nunca antes lo había hecho. El pelo mojado se adhería a la frente como su segunda piel.

El viento estaba a punto de soplar una bocanada de aire otoñal; el cielo, empapado de un azul frío. Volvió su rostro en dirección al pasto crecido y hacia el lago en la distancia, cambiando el paso sólo para saltar sobre la carrilera.

Aceleró el paso.

Pensó que si alcanzaba suficiente altura, agarraría el cielo. Por vez primera, sus ojos, rasgando la superficie del pasto, divisaron el más allá. A medida que subía, sus piernas empezaron a sentirse livianas. En el sol, sus ojos. Latigazos de fuego húmedo acariciaron su cara, formando lagunas en sus oídos.

Alzó los brazos. Atrapó el viento.

Sus pies dejaron la tierra.

Estaba libre.

Into the "Out" Door

My brother Enriqué always called my papa, "One crazy hombre." And, I would laugh. I think I was too young at that time to know what he meant. My papa would come home drunk. "He's stinkin' man—he's one crazy hombre."

Enriqué and I, at those stinky times, would stay in the room we shared, listening to him slap my mama around. "Where the hell is my supper?" And stuff like that. That's when Enriqué would say funny stuff to keep me from crying. He'd fall into roles from those old movies we'd always watched together. "Hey, amigo," he'd say in a bad Mexican accent, "Watch it. He got a gun." As the slapping and yelling got louder, so did Enriqué. Believe it or not those were my favorite memories. Enriqué and me in that room.

When my papa wasn't drunk all the time, and before he stopped coming home, my papa wasn't so bad. He even took me and Enriqué to the zoo once. "It's the German in him that's bad," my mama always said. "The German in him likes to drink." He was half German and half Puerto Rican. My mama was Mexican.

"Tell 'em you're Mexican, Luis," Enriqué told me when he was walking me to the first grade. Walking me when everyone else's mamas or papas were doing it.

"Why?" I asked him, because he was four years wiser than me. He looked at me with that smirk I was to hate him for later, a smirk he even wore when I had to ID his body at the morgue when he died from an overdose of too much something.

"Listen, *pendejito*," he cuffed me playfully behind the head, "just say what I tell you and life in school will be easier, okay?" He laughed. I liked his laugh. "A damn Mexigermanrican, man," he laughed. "Trust your bro." I liked him then a lot. And I listened to what he told me—then.

At school I told everybody, like Enriqué told me, that I was Mexican, not German, or Puerto Rican. Though I didn't look as dark as Enriqué did, because of my last name, León, they believed me. Not that it mattered much to first-graders, or the other kids from the neighborhood whose families were as mixed as mine. It was only when I went to high school that I found it was good to say I was Mexican.

When it was just Mama, Enriqué, and me at home, those were the best times. My papa worked down at the shipyards and never came home much. When my mama was happy, just before Enriqué used, the three of us would camp out on the old eating couch. We called it that because after you laid on it a while you felt as if it was eating you up. We'd pop us some corn and drink sodas and watch the late movies, especially on Fridays. We'd stay up all night jumping at every sound, thinking my papa was coming in. And if he did, Enriqué and I would run to our room and Mama'd pretend she was sleeping. No good 'cause he'd wake her, and then the stories would begin along with the yelling.

As Enriqué got older, those runs to our room and the yelling made his stories all the more angry. "If I was only another year older, and bigger, I'd kick his ass out of here," he said to me. The shouting was getting louder and he was getting angrier. "Listen, Luis, that crazy hombre is nothing but a drunk. I could push his ass down if he ever came at me," he said.

The older we got, the more it seemed we were fair game for Papa. "You lazy sumbitches," he'd say. "I'll give you what

for." He'd come at us and we'd stand there because we were
too scared to run. But I could see Enriqué wouldn't be scared
much longer. Papa'd slap at us, missing most of the time
because he was too drunk. We'd stand there taking it so
Mama didn't have to (Enriqué stepping up for more because
I was younger). We figured to give Mama a break—it didn't
really hurt because he was so drunk. And, anyway, he was
hardly ever coming home much then.

"He ain't much, Luis," Enriqué said to me. I was in
third grade and Enriqué was starting to stay out all night.
"Once when I was a kid we went down to the Pick 'N Save
and he went in the 'out' door—that's how wasted stupid he
is," Enriqué laughed.

When we went to the zoo that one time it was almost
great. It was before, I think, first grade—the summer before.
I was six and Enriqué was ten or eleven. It was great because
my papa was talking and was only half drunk. But we only
saw half the zoo. Then we saw the inside of a bar—almost
great. Enriqué taught me how to shoot pool, anyway.

By the time I was ten, Papa and Enriqué both weren't
hardly coming home. "It's the German in them," Mama'd
say. I tried to figure it out: if Papa was half, then Enriqué and
I were a quarter. I wondered how long until I felt that quarter in me. I wanted to ask Enriqué how, or when, he felt it.
Was it like a ball growing inside you that you don't know is
there until it's too late? And you'd need to drink to shrink
it? Enrique'd come home stinkin' sometimes, I could smell
Papa on him—the German in him. But he wasn't as bad.
Maybe because he was only a quarter, and I had hopes that
the other parts would save him. Then one night the quarter
and half met.

Enriqué was only a little drunk and he was telling me
about fishing. He was going to take me fishing some day.
Not like that crazy hombre who only took us to the zoo and
bar. "Fuck him," he said.

We heard Papa come in and start on Mama. I followed
Enriqué out to the living room. Mama was lying on the eating couch. "Go, Tolfio. We don't want you here. Why do you
come back?" Mama said.

"This is my house, bitch," Papa said and staggered
around the room, waving his hand around. "I pay the bills."

We stood a ways off and I could feel that this was the
time Enriqué would no longer be scared. "What're you two
sumbitches lookin' at?" Papa said, trying to stop his circling
the room, that arm still hanging out there like a one-winged,
drunken bird. We stood there and I was scared, not of him,
but of what I felt vibrating in the floor. It was coming from
Enriqué. That quarter in him was coming up and mixing
with the other parts and it was vibrating from him into me.

I looked at him. His face was so red, and his neck was
pounding. "C'mon 'Rique, let's go." I grabbed his arm. The
voltage of him shot straight into my toes. I felt like I was
inching above the floor. Papa found his feet and came over
to us swaggering. He was drawn to Enriqué—I could see it:
the half in him was being drawn. He stood a ways back and
put his fists on his hips.

"Sooo. . . " Papa said, drawing the words in the air in
front of us—and I could see every one of them. "You a fuck-
ing man, now?" He threw his head back and let out a long,
stinking laugh.

Enriqué just stared at him, red-faced and with pounding neck, and smiled.

"What're you looking at, boy?" Papa said, inching closer, attached to the floor like Enriqué was.

"My shit . . . but it can't be—I just flushed the toilet,"
he said. I was scared, but I still laughed. It was funny. I even
heard my mama laugh. Papa's face was confused for a second
in all that laughing. Enriqué wasn't laughing, either. Papa
kept his eyes on Enriqué and snaked out an arm and slapped

me hard in the ear. My head became hollow and I remember thinking, holy shit, he knocked my brain out.

Mama had stopped laughing and now it was Papa and Enriqué. Enriqué, I think, was fifteen and stood as tall as Papa, so they were eye to eye—laughing. "Why don't you hit me?" Enriqué said.

Papa still laughed and snaked out again and hit me in the same ear. I could feel blood trickling out. Still, my head emptying fast, I wanted to stay and watch. Enriqué stepped in fast and punched Papa on the chin. The quarter met the half and Papa fell flat on his ass—it looked as if the floor came up and spanked him. Enriqué kept moving and brought his foot up and kicked him in the face—flat.

Mama never got up.

Enriqué just stood there. And I felt the smile on my face.

"Go, Tolfio. And don't come back," Mama said quietly from the eating couch. He picked himself up and left. I remember thinking that we'll never go to the zoo again. That was the last time I saw my papa.

Enriqué was good for a while after that. He even tried to go to school every day. But that something inside of him was growing, and I could see it—growing fast and hard. It seemed to make his body bulge sometimes. And it must've hurt, too, because it was in his eyes like small red dots. He'd come home with a smell on him different than booze. He'd sit quietly for a long time, then he'd tap his feet on the floor as if he had bugs in his shoes and he was trying to stamp them dead.

He'd sit looking at the floor with his long black hair almost covering his face. I could sit there for hours and watch the colors move in and out of his face: deep red, to a quick white, and then a pinkish blue. Back and forth like our old TV. This was before he scared me too much. "'Rique? You sick, man?" I'd say.

"No, *pendejito*," he'd say back and grin. He'd quickly stand and pace the room. Mama'd look in sometimes and moan, "Mother Mary." But mostly she stayed in her room when Enriqué was home. Then sometimes he'd just sit there and grin a dreamy grin. He'd mutter to himself, "No sleep for the tappin' feet. No sleep for the tappin' feet." Over and over again.

"You're one crazy hombre, 'Rique," I told him, once, when he began his pacing. He was pacing and bouncing up and down as if he was a springman. He stopped and settled in the gravity and stared at me. "Luis, you better watch your mouth because . . ." he said, and never finished because he bounced out the door.

Mama came out of her room, sat next to me, and hugged me. "Don't make your brother mad, Luis. Okay?" she said.

"Okay, Mama," I promised her. I didn't mean to make him mad—I thought he'd find it funny.

On Friday nights it was just my mama and me watching the late night movies, snuggled on the eating couch with a bowl of buttered popcorn between us. And every time we heard a sound, we'd jump in fear, thinking Papa was coming home.

Invisible Green

It was Saturday and hot, and Fowler poked at his teeth with a toothpick in that lazy manner of his. "Hey, Fowler, man," I called from my bunk, watching him check the wide spaces between his teeth. "What color am I?"

"Green, Lionman," he drawled in the slow deliberate way that he had. "We're all green." Fowler was from Birmingham, Alabama, or the 'Bama as he drawled it. He was a slow, methodical black. He reminded me of those old-time movies me and my brother Enriqué used to watch as kids. The movies where the black's eyes were always bugged out, and then he'd say, "Whew, Mr. Benny, I's scared. Shorely am." And Enriqué and I'd go around saying, "Oooh, Mr. Man, I's scared. Shorely am." Except Fowler ain't no "late-night nigger," as he put it. He was just deliberate.

"Lionman, what's up? Let's go get us a soda, man. Cool your head."

He started calling me Lionman from the first day we met. "What's your name, man?" he had said. The toothpick, there, looking as if it always belonged.

"León, man. Luis." I said, holding out my hand. He looked at my hand as if it'd produce a knife or something. I started to get mad.

"Which is it?" he drawled real long, which shook me because of those old-time movies I'd seen. "León Luis, or

Luis León?" He took that toothpick in his mouth, and started to search his teeth for words.

I was hot. I was tired of the army, of Oklahoma, of the fuckin' bullshit triplet papers I'd signed and would sign again—I knew, again. I threw my duffel bag onto one of the two bunks in the room, hoping by chance that it was his. I was getting kicked out of the army and I wanted to kick something back. I eyed him hard. Not that I was a fighter like my brother Enriqué was, but I wasn't a runner either. I was ready. Fowler stood there eyeing me up and down. He was about my size, medium build, but there was something lightning-like beneath his green fatigues. He looked like he was coiled like a charming snake in a basket.

He held out a hand that looked like you'd wanna strike matches on it, and smiled around his toothpick. "Fowler," he drawled. Then, "You lookin' hot, Lionman, have a soda." I was a bit surprised he knew my last name meant 'lion' in English. He threw me a Coke from the small fridge in the room. These were the holding barracks and they were more like small apartments. He reclined back on the other bunk, deliberate-like, smacking his lips every time he drank from his Coke, and watched me unpack.

"Been here three weeks, man," he said to my back as I made my bunk up. "Seen too many go—exceptin' Fowler. Ain't that some pretty shit, man?" He laughed and the Coke made me feel cool.

"Three weeks? They told me, two, to process home," I said back. He didn't say anything to that because it was 'old-time-shit'—we both knew how fucked up the army was, and there was no need in my bitchin' on top of his. He had beat me to it, so I kept quiet. That was army protocol.

We were in what the others called the loser's squad. Because of one screwup or another we were going home—to the world. Sometimes it was a misdemeanor that you forgot to tell your recruiter about, or you had your appendix out a month before you came in. Sometimes it was because you were just too stupid to do even a push-up, or maybe there were too many of "us" in at the same time and it made someone nervous. But you didn't ask the "why?" You were told.

"Yeah, man. Cool my head," I said back, thinking about moving my legs to get up. Because I knew Fowler, once he decided on something—it was done already. There was no use in my hurrying. It just happened, slow, on its own.

I joined the army because I had no place to go. My mama became sick and had to go stay with my tía in Chicago. But I wasn't invited. I was seventeen and kicked out of school, and I hung too much with the neighborhood. My tía said, "Go in the army. They'll take you, educate you. Maybe even make a man out of you—'cause you ain't coming here, *comprende?*" I guess she thought I was too much like my brother was, or my papa. Except I didn't do drugs like Enriqué did, and my papa, well, who knew where that bastard was. I hadn't seen him since I was about eleven, and then only when he was drunk.

My papa would come home to give us "what for" as he said, and we'd take our turns at a beating. But the beatings usually didn't hurt because he was too drunk.

I was deciding which leg I wanted to move—left or right. I said, "Fowler, if I ain't Mexican or white, what am I?"

"Invisible," he said, getting to his feet.

When I'd first hit boot camp, I blended in with the rest of the Oklahoma scenery—dry and hot as the other newbees. We lined up together to get our uniforms, all with that same look on our faces: some came from Detroit, some from Chicago, some from New York—later I'd asked Fowler if he'd ever been to New York, and if he had, would he have missed it? All's he did was laugh. "Shiiit."

Then we all collected our hair together on the same floor, and laughed at each other, except the big black dude from LA. He looked as if his hair jumped off and no one was going to ask how, or laugh at that dude. We gathered for our first meal, our uniforms looking as if we weren't men enough to fit into them. Drill sergeants swarmed the tables like hungry ants, sayin' shit about how our mothers raised "sloths." "Don't eyeball me. Don't eyeball me, boy. Don't eyeball me, shit-for-brains." They walked the tables, slinging their words at us like whips—and they felt like whips, too. We all left our first meal hunched over, but at least we looked the same.

We walked out of our billet and headed for the soda machine on the opposite side of the HQ building. They had put the machine right in front of where we were supposed to line up every morning for roll call.

"Temptation of your better sensibilities," our drill sergeant said in his southern twang. He pointed to the soda machine. "There, maggots, is what you have to earn—the luxuries of the world." He was an ex-Green Beret who limped from too much shrapnel in his leg from 'Nam. He was a crazy sumbitch who'd as soon spit on you as look at you, as he told us every chance he could.

"That, girls," he continued to point at the machine, "is what you will die for." And then he got real cold in his face, even though we were sweating our nuts off. "Coca-fuckin'-cola is, from now on," then he screamed, "God and country."

We screamed back, all one for a moment. "Yes, Drill Sergeant."

We walked up to that machine, passing by the groups of GIs that had formed almost from the first week of boot. Groups of just blacks, Puerto Ricans, Mexicans, Asians, whites, Filipinos who I thought were Asian, but were different somehow.

"Fowler," a black dude yelled. "Why don' you hang with the brothers, brother?"

Everyone was looking at us. I recognized a couple of the Mexicans, but they turned away as soon as I caught their eyes. I think everyone was looking because they knew we were going for a soda—something they couldn't have. They were still Army, and we were going home. No longer in the game. The blacks thought it cool Fowler could have something nobody else could have, but they didn't like the idea that I was having the same thing.

Fowler stopped, in his casual way, hands in his pockets, and stared at the dude that said it. His buddies were slappin' fives, high, low, to the sides, and laughing at me. What could I do? Kick ten dudes' asses? "What, man?" Fowler drawled back their way, pulling his toothpick out to make room for his voice.

"I said, why you hangin' with a no-man? The spics don't even hang with him. Hang with us, brother." The dude went on laughing, I could feel my ears getting hot and red. I wanted to go—go to that soda machine.

"Hey, man, that's not cool." Fowler shook his head, pronouncing sentence on that dude.

"What? You too good for us, brother?" the dude drawled back, trying to imitate Fowler in a bad way.

"Brother? You my brother? Was your mother my mother? Give me some money, then, motherfucker." Fowler drawled and pronounced sentence on them all. "C'mon, Lionman, we got a Coke waitin'. I'm hot—need a coolin'."

We walked away, not saying anything at all.

One of the first things they drilled into us was that we were now all the same—there were no more spics, niggers, chinks, dagos, kikes, or whatever words we could think of to call each other—we were only green. "In the sun, maggots, you're all green on the outside, and red meat on the inside!" they screamed at us, into us, until we screamed back, "Yes, Drill Sergeant."

I got used to the groups, and not fittin' in. The Mexicans called me "gringo" because I wasn't as dark as my brother Enriqué was, and the whites, well, I wasn't. So I found a place with Fowler and the 'Bama.

I still felt hot in the ears, and Fowler knew it. He was quiet for a while, searching his brain for the thing to say. Something that would cool me like a Coke. I knew we had to go back the same way, and he knew it, too. To go another way was to be a chickenshit. "Lionman, they're just words. Don't mean a thing," he said.

We got our Cokes and headed back. This was the platoon's day off and I guess it was just too hot to waste it on us. The groups had moved around like some big dance and now the Mexicans were closest as we passed. I saw one of the guys I used to know, and he turned away again. That was cool, I thought. The sun was just too hot. We went back into our billet because we had a fan.

"Fowler says, he's got a week left." Fowler smacked on his Coke.

"Yeah, man. I bet," I said. I wondered if he was ever going home, or if he was just lying to me. I had been there two weeks and he was still there. There was a knock at our door.

"C'mon in man," Fowler said, neither one of us wanting to get up. A dude from our lost squad came in. He also was waiting to go home. He had a bad knee. We all took turns running errands for the Drill Sergeant in Charge of Quarters. They had us running for them on twenty-four-hour shifts because we "had nothing better to do anyway."

"León, man. Your paperwork came through. You're going home Monday," he said trying to catch his breath.

I was mad because he told me in front of Fowler. "You ran over here just for that," I said around my Coke.

"No, but I thought you'd wanna know, man," he said.

"Thanks." I toasted my can to him.

"Yeah, right," he mumbled and left.

I drank my Coke in the silence that he'd left for us. I didn't look at Fowler—I didn't want to see his face.

"Lionman is goin' home—that's some pretty shit, man," Fowler laughed. "Here's to ya, man." I heard the Coke slosh in his can. I looked at him then. He was holding his can up to me in a salute.

"Yeah, right. . . ," I said—what could I say? I could feel the blood in my face. I knew he could too. "Maybe your papers are there, too," I said, not really believing it.

"Naw, man. They want to keep this ol' black ass around to run errands for them. You all will go and it'll just be Fowler." He sighed and sipped at his Coke.

"My mama's sick," I said.

"So's mine," he said, seriouslike. Then he roared, "Yeah, man. Sick of being black." He went on laughing.

"You think so?" I said, meaning a lot of things—but he knew what I meant.

"Don't play that shit with me, Lionman," he drawled.

"What?" I knew.

"The army don't see no color but green. It's only us that sees . . . No, we're invisible." He stopped and sat on the edge of his bunk, holding his Coke in his hands as if it was a tiny bird. His long, black fingers twirled the can around and around. I studied my own can.

"Then why are you here?" I said, taking a chance on our friendship.

"Same as you, man. No place to go."

"No," I said, sitting up and moving to the edge of the bunk. "Why are you *still* here?"

He stopped moving his Coke around and began to study me. "You know? You're a pretty smart *boy*. Sitting here, for all this time, wondering why a nigger like me is goin' and not yet gone. Still, you never asked the 'why?'" he laughed, shaking his head.

"None of my business," I said.

He stared at me—his eyes like black marbles. "Naw," he said and lay back down, unfolding himself like a dark piece of paper. "Where ya goin', when you gets there?"

"Milwaukee," I said. "My mama is in Chicago with my tía, but wants to come home—to our house. Ain't much." I shrugged and stretched back out, watching Fowler between my feet.

"Home," Fowler said. "Nice to have a home. I'll go back to the 'Bama, man."

"Why?"

"No where else to go, man. Haven't you been listening?" he said.

"No, why are you getting kicked out?" I said, afraid he'd get mad. Instead, he grunted. I was quiet, giving him time to answer.

"You'll go home. You have a house. I'll go back to Birmingham. We have a house, too." His voice sounded distant to me—as if he were disappearing into that bunk. "It's just you and your mama. There are seven in my house—can't even wiggle your feet for scratchin' someone else's back."

"My brother's dead," I said. "We're poor, too."

"Man, you ain't white. You ain't Mexican. You ain't black. Come live in the 'Bama, man. There you poor," he laughed from deep in his bunk. "There, you have to be invisible. If you ain't white, you scared." He drawled and became still.

I glanced between my feet to make sure he was still there.

"Don' worry about it Lionman . . . it's all the same in the finish. Underneath we all the same—you heard the song. It'll make you hot . . . "

"Yeah," I laughed. "Shore 'nuff."

"Now you got it!" he said. I could feel him smiling, though I wasn't looking. "Anyway, man. What makes you think I'm in a hurry to get home?"

Laundromat Blues

I'm in this laundromat, and my mama still nags me, so I come here to get away and do a little wash. I gotta get away from her. The fuckin' laundromat. This Chicano kid, maybe fifteen, comes in. I see him as he holds his coat tight around him—hands in the pockets. He's cold so he comes here to be warm. Except he looks strung—real strung. Ants probably crawling on his arms and legs, making him dance. He looks at me quick as if I licked his face with my eyes. He shivers and goes to check the next room. No one is there. Only here, in this room: just me, an old Hispanic woman, a fat white woman, two black boys (about eight and ten) and a black man. The Chicano kid pulls a gun.

A fuckin' gun. In here, the laundromat. I want to go over and tell him how stupid he is to rob a laundromat. If people had money they'd wash and dry at home. Stupid. He waves the gun like a big black finger. I stop folding, sliding my new jeans out of view. Jack-up the Liquor Mart next door, I want to tell him—tell him again, how stupid. But I realize that wouldn't do, he'd jack me.

I begin to make up stories, like I did when we had to ID my brother Enriqué's body. I was like twelve. Enriqué was cold, too, that day. Mama sent out Hail Marys bouncin' down the hall. "Go see to your brother, Luis."

Maybe the kid with the gun could be Enriqué. "Luis, man." He'd come to me shaking, holding the gun up so's not to plug me. "Luis, I'm cold, man."

"Shit," I'd tell him. "Quit the shit, Enriqué. You're blue already, man."

"Luis, I need bad. Luis, I need real baddd. . . ." He'd shake his teeth at me. "You got?—no? Any cash? Are you holdin'?"

I'd then hold up my hands, empty, as my pockets and life. "No, man. Tapped out." But he's not my brother, and he's hungry for something—cash, not stories.

"Cash," he yells. The two women—one old, one white, and black guy, eye him like he shouted, "God!" Maybe the heavy white woman with the orange hair will scream. He'll glide up to her on his need—glide up to her rippling in his shoes. "Shut the fuck up, bitch!" He'll stroke the barrel of the gun through her orange mop—gently. "Mama," he'll say, a choke in his throat. Then, "Bitch." She'll fall to the floor with a gash across her forehead.

The two black boys stare at the gun—wondering, I bet, if it's real. When we first moved into our neighborhood I was twelve, and my mama sent me to get eggs. Two blacks stopped me. "Let's see it," one said—the one with big teeth.

"What?" I knew. My money. The one with little teeth pulled up his shirt to show me the gun against his dry belly.

"You carrin' man? You spics always carry." He pinched his lips at me.

"Nothin' better than that." So I gave the money over. Then they disappeared as if the neighborhood opened its mouth and swallowed them. I hoped it choked.

"Useless!" Mama said. "*Pendejo.*" She sent me back. I never carried a knife—everyone carried a gun. We could hardly afford eggs.

But the woman with the orange hair didn't scream, and the kid with the gun, instead, goes through the old woman's purse. He finds a couple dollars, a handful of quarters, and then pushes the old woman's purse off the folding table. She shrugs her shoulders. She is old; old enough to understand a few wrinkled bills and odd change aren't worth it. And she's smart enough to leave her money at home; smart enough and poor enough already not to miss it. She probably woke this morning in her long underwear, because the heat's not too good in her boxed palace. The landlord huddles near the furnace, she figures, blowing out the pilot light. The good thing about the winter, she smiles, is that the cockroaches have gone south to Mexico. When she was a child in Mexico City, she and her four brothers would sweep the cockroaches out of their upper flat into the barrio, watching the black rain clatter to the hot garbage on the street. Then they went out to beg, so's they didn't have to eat cockroaches later for supper.

The kid dumps her life onto the floor and still the old woman shrugs—not smiling or hating, just looking into that big hot Mexico sun; the same sun that probably made her father's body steam when he dropped dead in the street from too much cheap tequila; the hot sun that made her mother squint to make sure it was their father, and then turn away to make supper at home.

The kid eyeballs the old woman, hesitating in his itch. Maybe he sees in her the *abuela* that was once his, shrugging her shoulders when he asked her where *his* papa was. "*No se, mijo.*" Her eyes looking like the Mexican summers, too. She doesn't know where his mother is either. No one does. His *abuela's* face looks like his mother's did.

He raises the gun to his chest, level with the old woman's face. He wants to hit her. I can see that. But, instead he kicks the pieces of her life around the laundromat. The fuckin' laundromat.

He spins away on his rippling feet and goes to the black man, not me. He's saving me for last. The man flinches, looks to the two black boys—yeah, they're with him. The black boys don't look back. They still watch the gun.

One of the black man's hands, the right one, moves toward his back pocket as if he's going for his six-shooter like John Wayne. Except it's his wallet—stupid move, he's thinking as he does it; his hand goes back to his just-cashed paycheck. Just cashed and counted: $75 to fix his car, $50 to keep the heat on, fuck the phone, $30 for a night out, maybe $25 more for some blow—powder the nose; the rest, if any, for groceries. Except now, he's pushing more toward groceries. And maybe a little more to put new shoes on his boys' feet. He fucked up and it's on his face. The kid's floating on lightning bolts and doesn't miss shit—he knows the black is holding, and from the black's face, holding big.

The black will stare at the cops, later, as they write down what happened. "Fucker took it all . . . how am I supposed to pay the heat? phone? Shit, my car needs fixin' . . . what, I ride the bus?"

The two white cops will look at each other—knowingly. Smiling. "What about the night out and the Peruvian powder, huh? Don't bullshit us—we know you people." But they won't say that, instead they'll smirk and say, "We'll get back to you." *When hell freezes over and lets in white men because hell is an all black neighborhood—nigger!*

The kid becomes almost calm. His face glows. The gun points at the black's head, almost lovingly. The two black boys' mouths drop in excitement, and hunger, too. "Keep going for it, man." The kid's lips follow the words as if they're stuck to them—like blowing a kiss. The black reaches back for it, pulls it out as if the wallet betrayed him by not being a gun—for John Wayne being white and his night out is in his hand (fuck the heat bill) and he sees the Colombian nose candy march across his fingers as he hands the wallet over to the kid.

The wallet disappears into the pocket of the kid's coat to stay warm—warm cash, he's thinking. The laundromat becomes silent, the dryers even are soundless as they spin out the quarters put into them. The woman with orange hair and the old woman sigh in hopes that the animal has been fed and now it will leave; hope the need is met also, but you can never be sure. The hunger that's inside this kid with a gun is unsure—he's robbing a laundromat. Stupid. But I don't say so because it will be my turn soon.

The kid licks his lips, tasting already the cure, the ointment, for his itch. He grabs the arm that's holding the gun around the elbow. Through the coat he feels the spots that are waiting—needing. He's thinking of going now, but he's on fire. He looks to me, so's I flinch. Now his eyes lick that fire across my face.

"Enriqué," I want to say. "Go, man. You've worn your welcome. Man, it's a laundromat!" But he's not Enriqué; he's not dead—yet. He's alive with what my mama called an unholy fire. She'd yell at Enriqué, *"No eres mijo! Eres el hijo del diablo."*

He'd grin at that and say, "I didn't know you slept with the devil, Mama."

The kid could be my brother—he scares me now. Enriqué would come home shaking like this kid, blue as he was when I ID'd him; blue angel, Mama called him. "Luis," he'd say when he wasn't blue, and didn't itch. "Walk in the street at night—stay in the lights. Remember, he who sleeps in the streets never wakes." His hand was always wiping his mouth as if words dribbled out and down his chin like lazy syrup.

The kid holds on to his pocket as he comes to me—sure in his score. Both hands are full and I wonder if he'll grow another. *"Hermano,* what do you have for me?" he smiles the smile of Mexico—of the sun. The family.

"*Nada.*" I pull out my pockets and hold my hands up. "*Hermano.*" I can't help how the word tastes like shit as I say it. He hears.

"Come." He stops a ways from me—close, but not too close. "It's payday from Tío Sam. Skip the food stamps, *hermano.* Give the money." He smiles at his little joke, but his eyes become black like the gun he's holding. Go, Enriqué! I want to shout. Go back to the morgue. Run before death catches you and brings you home. I want to punch his face because he looks like Enriqué.

"Luis," Enriqué had said. "We'll go fishing one day. Just you and me." He was sixteen that day and I was nine—almost a year before I had to see him at the morgue; a year before he started to look like he used—before blue. "Fishing on the big lake—no bullshit fish." Mama yelled at him rarely then, because he stayed out late—missed school. "Man, Luis, I have this friend with a big boat. He'll take us out, when it's warmer. We'll catch big no bullshit fish," he'd laugh. He was always laughing, then.

"Man, I don't have no money." I wave my hands at the kid—nothing there, see? He looks at me long, it seems. There is no more time. I don't even know how long he's been here. Maybe forever. I lick my lips, like I used to do when Enriqué was home and he was high, and I was afraid.

"You got what you need—*hermano,*" I whisper to him. "Go." I look at the others, they are all in their own places, too, because it's me and not them any more. I'm just like him, they're thinking. It would serve me right if he plugged me—we're all the same anyway—the black knows this. The woman with the orange hair—fat orange hair—is white and poor, too, but still is white. The old woman knows the kid and me, because she's the same, but the sun blinds her from home and the kid and I are different from her.

The kid's black eyes stop for a second. Thinks it over—his brain must be on overdrive because his forehead seems to bulge as he thinks. Enriqué would look like that, too. "Fishing," he'd slur and wipe his mouth, his face—changing his smile into a clown's face and back again—then back— then back. "Wanna fishh . . . Luis? Big fuckin' no bullshit fish . . . " He'd swipe his face, dribble his words. "Big boat on a big lake with big fish." He'd laugh until I cried and Mama threatened to call the police. "Police?" His lips seemed too big for words. It was hard for him to speak. "Po-lice. *Policia.* Don' come in this neighborhood—need no fuckin' badges here." He'd laugh himself out the door. I cried, Mama swore to God.

The kid's still thinking. The last of the dryers stops. The two black boys edge around for a better look at the gun pointed at me. Later they will hope to say they saw him (me) shot. Be on the ten o'clock news—"Yup, shot his ass dead. His own kind." They will tell how big the gun was; how it jumped in the kid's hand like it was a living breath-ing thing that sneezed; how my eyes turned up to God and exploded; how the kid laughed at his own as he ran away.

"Don't," I say, as I would say "excuse me." "Go while you can. Run." He wipes his mouth and heads for the back door he came in. He moves slowly at first, as if he's unsure where he is going. His face pushes the others away from his path out. The gun disappears into his other coat pocket. But his face, eyes, lips, hold everyone back—even the black who wants his wallet; who feels again that it is his kind that always loses, and nobody else. The kid looks at me, and if he says "we'll go fishin' one of these days," I'll scream—I know it. The back door opens and the cold takes him back into its arms, and I can see them. I can see them, and they're blue.

"No Sleep for the Tappin' Feet"

I can only imagine how it was for him: living on the edge of something that was waiting to swallow you—cruising the streets. But keeping me and Mama safe. That was Enriqué. He held me in his arms, so much older than me and yet only by four years; years that felt like forever over a short distance in his arms. A circle. Don't cry, Luis, he'd say, someone will hear you. Someone. Someone who can't smile and smells of cheap tequila, or whiskey, or even beer. Someone who just smells cheap.

He, the street, tells his story to me. Not rumors—Truth. I sit on the steps of our small house. Across the street, the houses are dead—windows boarded up with wood and memories no one wants.

"No sleep?" that's what Mister Jones says. Laroy Temper Jones. I call him Jones. When I'm out, and needin', I say, "La-roy, I'm Jonesin'. Can you help me, brother?" And he says back, slick as oil on a fish's skin, "You got the cash, man, I got the trash." He's not really my friend, he just fronts me when I'm low. "Man, that horse riding you good?" he says, smiling his lips at me and blowing through them like a horse. "I got some rock—do you good, man."

"No, man, I'm already burnin'—need to slow down," I say back.

"Ah, man, no sleep for the tappin' feet, huh?" He produces a bag. I hold out my hands, empty as my pockets. "Oh,

'Rique man . . . by Friday or this gate's closed for business." I know it won't be, 'cause I'm a "valued consumer." I do pay, but my lines are runnin' out. I lost my job, my mama hides her money too good, blah blah blah . . . fuck it. I just get it somehow and I get. Jones knows I'll be workin' for him soon and I know it too—so he gives and I get. I take. And I can't stop.

Shit, sometimes it passes the time. I mean it ain't as if I'm drooling on myself, or stinkin' like three-day garbage— or sleepin' in it. I just have this growth inside me that hurts, and the horse rides it away. Jones cuts me a quarter. Hands it to me. He thinks of doin' the carrot and stick thing on me— I see it in his eyes—but he don't. He knows better. "Man, I can get you some work. And discounts, 'Rique . . . " He knows me, and he's afraid.

Most people are afraid of me, but I don't see why. I mean, hey, I'm doin' my trip, it's just no one better stop my ETA or they'll be DOA. My little brother, Luis, is even afraid of me. I see the look in his eyes that we shared when we watched our old man beat up our mama. I don't like it! I ain't that piece of shit. If I'm stringin', I just stay away from home. But sometimes I need what's there . . . so I can't help it. My mama don't speak to me no more. She just ridin' out the shit, I figure. First the old man, now me—just ridin' out the shit.

I grab the bag out of Laroy's chocolate hand—candy hand. "No man," I tell him, starin' him upside his face, even though my eyes are sinkin'. I feel it. "I do. And that's all I do."

"Suit yourself, man," he grunts—he knows. "Don't come back to me if you ain't scratchin' my palm with some dead white dudes Friday." He flashes his teeth to me in what he thinks will chill me. I flash back—"Yeah right!"

I take my stuff and jag myself up. I only do enough to keep me centered in gravity. Later, for more. I love the streets at night. People hangin' in the shadows, like dark tigers waiting to spring on you. Rip your throat open. Then they see it's me—that I'm marked as one who don't take shit—they thinkin' maybe he's packin', or if he ain't, then he one crazy motherfucker. I pack all sorts of surprises on me. I run with the tigers sometimes myself—roll someone stupid enough to wander my jungle, but nothing heavy. I don't, yet, sell junk, or jack liquor marts, or any of that stupid shit. Ain't enough there to want to spend time doin' time.

I come up Thirty-Fifth Street and cut down Cherry. Our house sits back a ways from the street. Not like those flats that crowd the street. We have it all to ourselves. My old man inherited it from some dead relative who must not have known what a fuckin' shit he was. I showed him what for, and kicked his drunken ass right out of the house. Even if I don't always go home, I watch—watch to make sure he don't come 'round. I put the word out on the street, and he knows it. The street talks, and I listen.

I first shot a guy when I was twelve—four years ago. It wasn't really nothin', man. I mean I took off his kneecap with a twenty-two pistol. Sumbitch had a knife. It was this twisty lookin' big white dude that hung out in the hood. He'd buy from Laroy, or whoever was holdin' that day, and hang. The tigers let him hang as long as he shared what he was buyin'—then it was cool. Me, I come up wearin' my old man's trench coat, red bandanna around my head. Hey, man, I was twelve. I thought I was supposed to look like an LA *vato*. This dude, he was tokin' some rock, and he must've been havin' the dancin' feet. "Hey, man, a fuckin' pinto beaner," he laughed at me.

I don't know, but I think the brothers thought he was done sharin' his stuff because they didn't stop him. They knew me for comin' tough from the shoulders. At twelve, even, I was good with my hands. And because the old man had some Deutschland in him, I wasn't exactly pint-sized. They stepped back from him, blowin' the last of the dude's smoke right in his face as if in farewell. I learned young—real young, that you didn't talk your game. Not like on TV and shit, where the dude's always tellin' you how he's goin' to straighten your face for you. So I stepped in quick, head down as if I was goin' to cough, bringing my right shoulder down, then coming up. I snapped his head back quicklike, with a right to his jaw—a reminder of respect. I didn't try to hurt him because if I wanted, I could've busted his jaw—put him sleepy time.

The brothers laughed, applauded my restraint—hey, man, the dude was a consumer. But the dude came back out of his coat with a blade. Six inches. "Look man," one of the brothers said, "he pullin' out his dick." I jumped back. I had found my old man's .22 a couple days before and started to carry it for just such happenings.

"Fuckin' beaner," the dude said, "Gonna cut you, now." Like I said, man, don't talk. I figured this dude was from the east side or something. Watched a lot of TV. Well, I just pulled that pistola out and shot his kneecap off—well, sort of—just put a hole in his leg, anyway. The brothers stopped their laughin', Laroy came up to me, seriouslike. "Kid, disappear. We don't see shit. Exceptin' some white dude bleedin' to death, who better find someone else's sidewalk to bleed on, or he be bleedin' for real." The white dude took the hint and limped away. I didn't say a word from the time I walked up to the time I left. Like I says, the tigers don't ever fuck with me.

I walk myself through the streets, feelin' the eyes on my body—my gravity. It is quiet. I sit across on a dead house's stoop—watchin'. "Our home," Mama said. "This is a home." Yeah, right, when that crazy hombre got his ass kicked out it was—and when I left. But it stays a home because of me. Fuck 'em. I settle into my feet and watch the lights in the window: Luis, Mama. It is getting colder and Milwaukee winters are too cold for my ass. Maybe I'll go out to LA where I can get me some steady supply and work.

I ain't workin' for Mister Jones. He is small-time. Back when I was twelve, Jones was making a living—I thought he was cool, but now—shit, man, the tigers are runnin' in packs, drivin' big cars, and carryin' shit that could put a zipper in you with a quick pull of the trigger. The neighborhood's dyin'. Cocaine is boardin' up windows. People have gone crazy in the hood. Across from Mama's all the people we once knew have gone: Samudios moved on, Johnsons split—crack movin' in. Time soon for me, too.

My feet start to tappin', reminding me it's time to fix my gravity—pull myself to earth again. I want to go over and go in. I want to tell Mama that I can change, as the neighborhood's changed—but for better. I want to go into my room and tell Luis it's okay, man, I'd never hurt him or Mama; I want to take him fishin'. I could fix it. I know a dude with a big boat, who wants me to run his rock—put Laroy out of business. Put him against a wall—small fuckin' time pimp that he is. Hookin' every dude in the neighborhood. Business, he calls it. I could push some big rock, put my own pack together—rule this fuckin' desert—push into downtown. I could fix it.

My feet start to move on their own, and I can't sit any more. I can fix it, but first I need to fix myself.

To Say Good-bye

"From the moment I was born," said Florentino Ariza, "I have never said anything I did not mean."

The Captain looked at Fermina Daza and saw on her eyelashes the first glimmer of wintry frost. Then he looked at Florentino Ariza, his invincible power, his intrepid love, and he was overwhelmed by the belated suspicion that it is life, more than death, that has no limits.

—Gabriel Garcia Marquez,
Love in the Time of Cholera

Luis turned the last page, as he imagined his father turning the last page. It never crossed his mind that his father couldn't read. It was only important that he, who was gone for so long, turn it. In the same book. Luis lay the book down and this was the story that he made for himself; the only one he could tell, or believe.

His father closes the book and a tear is caught at the corner of his left eye. He wipes it away. Maybe it is the dusty lighting that makes his eye water. Not the memory of his own "Fermina" that he has left so long ago. He pushes himself out of his one chair, in his one-room efficiency that costs him almost all of his Social Security to pay for it each month, and goes for his last beer—*cerveza más fina!* The book he has found, in tatters, at the Salvation Army store; the same store he bought the weak lamp at—time and money later to replace the bulb. The cold beer tastes like wine and old memories.

It was here in his story that Luis smiled, sadly, yes, but still smiled as he told that part over and over in his mind. He could even see the one room as he imagined it to be all his life. The room had gotten smaller as he had gotten older. At first, his father had three rooms, one less than he and his brother and mama shared. Then, when his brother died, and it was just his mama and him, then his father's rooms got smaller—as their lives had.

His father is sixty-five and dead, living only on that last page that he turns over and over again, and cries. His Rosalita, he hears, from a vision maybe, has been dead this last year. From a cancer of some sort, and has floated above him to watch the tiredness with which he moves around his apartment. The voices that come through the wall late at night remind him of the violence he has played upon his own. His own Rosalita. Never mind the children, they have, and will, play out their own violence upon themselves. His friends rarely come to visit, because he has so few, so few. They are all violent as he is violent, therefore they can't find his heart, either. Or home. He has never heard that one of his own sons is dead, dead from a different type of loneliness he can't ever share. Only Rosalita with her dead cancer sees him. He had left her ten years ago and can't stop thinking.

Luis looked through his mother's things for pictures of his father. None could be found. He only remembered the drunken stinkiness of the man. He had never thought much of him until his mama passed away. He wanted to find something about his father that resembled happiness, but he couldn't, and wanted to hold that out from himself, at a distance, and cry for her. His mother left with her brother to die in another place.

Even that, her death, was denied to him.

She turned to him just before she left the small house they shared together. *"Mijo?"* she said.

"Yes, Mama?" he said.

"This is yours." She opened her arms, encompassing the room.

"Are you not coming back?"

"No," she said and left with her brother—his uncle, who didn't even say a word to him. Not even good-bye.

His uncle's family lived up north, in Neenah. An Indian word for water, he'd heard. They had a small house, but would be able to take care of her better, *mijo.* There was a small boy there—his cousin who he had seen once or twice at the few family get-togethers. The boy was twelve. The same age Luis was when he was left alone with just his mama. Mama called the boy "the sun." "He shines, Luis! Bright, like *el sol!"* she said every time she saw the boy. She moved her hands in large circles.

His father moves slowly between the time he closes the book and rises, to pacing his life out in the circles of his room. His father cannot know the abandonment Luis feels. First him, next Enriqué, and then his mother—are not the reasons the same? Luis wanted his father to think these things. The summer is closing and his father is hoping for a weak winter—the heat bills have killed him in the past. One more winter like the last and he will just sleep in the cold and die.

He had talked to his mother a month before she died. He didn't even know she was that close. She hid even that from him. "Luis," she said, and not "my boy." "I can't see any more, Luis."

"What?" he said, confused by the distance of her voice, not her words.

"I haven't seen in a long time, now. I can hardly hear anymore," she shouted. "But I am happy—the sun is here. That boy can fly!"

"What?" he said, again. No need to make sense out of her words anymore, he thought. "*Yo te quiero, Mama.*"

"I love you too, Luis." Not, my son.

Luis hung up the phone. He didn't know exactly where his mama was—only a number to talk occasionally, and yet, he didn't even know she was dead when he talked to her.

Stories, his father likes, too. Stories about lost love, found again, later: his Rosalita who floats above his bed every night. In silence. She with the misty face. It could be any ghost, but he knows it is her. He buys cheap tequila and drinks straight from the bottle as he had seen his own father do. The summer floats in his room like cheap tequila, and the extra money saved from the bills buys *mucho*. He drinks the day into the next and spills tequila on the book that lies opened to the last page on the floor.

The story of his mother's death came from a boy. "My tía, your mama, has died," the small voice said.

"Who is this?" he said.

"Dameon."

"When did my mama die?"

"My tía died today," he said, and hung up.

The house, paid with his and his mother's sweat, was now his alone, and he was only thirty. It wasn't much. But with the pizzeria, it would be enough. Anyway, in this neighborhood, *mijo*, who would you sell to? And who ever heard of a Mexican pizzeria?

His father's, mother's, and brother's voice, all the same anyhow. When he had told his mama he and Tomas were to be partners in the pizzeria, she had clucked her tongue and waved her arms, "You are not mortgaging this house, our home." She had truly believed that's what he wanted when he told her of the pizzeria. She had fear in her eyes that he'd ask her to do something like that. He was twenty when he and Tomas went into business together, and for that many years he had lived with his mother's fear of his father, his brother—and the fear that he was no different.

"No, Mama," he said. "We are taking out a small business loan. I am a veteran."

She clucked her tongue again. "Save your money and find a wife." He smiled. He had been out of the army for three years, sweeping floors for someone else. "Someone else's dust, amigo," Tomas had said. "Man, you and I can sweep our own dust and make pizzas."

Tomas became his brother when they were both twelve, playing in an old corrugated fort they had made behind the old slaughterhouse. This is how Luis tells it to the silence:

Tomas and Luis wish they were brothers. Luis wants Tomas as a brother because his own brother does drugs, and that scares him. Tomas is as lonely as Luis. Inside their fort made of corrugated metal, behind an abandoned building, they pretend they are brothers—not blood brothers, yet, because knives scare Luis also. They pretend they are on the run from the immigration into the US. They are both ten. Inside the fort of corrugated metal they build a fire out of old newspapers to keep warm, and they are careful not to make it too big, so the Migra man won't see. Tomas has brought stale tortillas, and Luis has the jalapeño peppers he took from home in his pocket.

"If we were brothers, Tomas," Luis says as he heats a tortilla over the flame, "I would let you pick the best tortilla." He is careful he doesn't burn his fingers.

"If we were brothers, I wouldn't take it." Tomas cuts up the peppers with his penknife, as he'd heard his father did when he came to the US. And how he figured his father did when he went back to Mexico, never to come back.

The flame gets too high and Luis pulls out some of the newspaper to lower it. They are afraid of the police finding them, too. But Luis's brother says the police don' come in their neighborhood, anyway. "If we were brothers, I would run first so they would only catch me," Luis says, as he stomps out some of the burning newspaper.

"No, we'd go together."

The tortillas are warm and Luis divides them up on a napkin on the dusty ground. Tomas divides up the jalapeño slices: three tortillas and six pepper slices each.

They fold up the peppers in the tortillas, two slices to each, and put out the fire. They eat in the dark as Tomas's father must have when he came, and when he went back. "If we were brothers, Luis, we'd never go back." Tomas holds out his tortilla.

"Never." Luis touches his own tortilla to Tomas's.

Luis knows his father could never understand brothers—his father's own brother in Neenah not having anything to do with him. And because of that, Luis's uncle has no use for Luis either. Then his other uncle takes away his mama, as maybe once his own father took away his mama from her family. His mama's family never had any use for his father, or Luis for that matter.

The summer is closing and the bottles of beer and tequila adorn the small apartment in stale remembrance. The ghost of Rosalita shines in the corner as his father sulks back into his one chair, with one leg straight out in front of him as if to run. His throat is dry and he wants to ask

Rosalita where the money for his next bottle will come from. But he can't form the words in her brightness.

Luis felt the part of his mama shining would be enough to last his story through one more telling. One more time Luis would read *Love in the Time of Cholera*, then maybe the story would fill with his own loneliness. He began at the end once more, and the light from his own lamp gave the words shadows. So Luis decided to remember his life in the book.

II.
An Absence of Place

Cerca de Aquí

I've wanted directions,
Direcciones.
A place I've searched for
where voices and people come together,
like the four corners
Utah, Colorado, Arizona and New Mexico.
Cuatro ángulos.
Like my life overlapping all the borders,
Sitio converger.
     Muy simple, no?
But I find my way so slowly
toward that place.
     Hablo despacio, por favor.
Each language so new.
Each people.
     Estoy buscando
I am looking.
Can you tell me
¡Es cerca de aquí?

Kimberly Blaeser

Cerrar la Puerta

I am the earth. The mountains, brown in their splendor, rise above the water. "Close the door, Sylvia," her mama was yelling. In their splendor they point towards the heavens, and God. "I'm wet already, Mama," Sylvia called back. The steam rising from the water mingled with the angry voice from below. The garden is fertile. My grass grows deep in the valley. I am ready.

She thought of Stefan from Spanish class—his eyes were like the sky. She thought of the thunder as the Spanish words that rolled off her friend Niss's tongue.

"Pendeja." Mama appeared at the door. "Close this damn door when you bathe."

"Yes, Mama," she whispered. The door slammed shut. She cupped her breasts, pushing them higher in the water. The soapy water slid down the sides over her fingers. The earth heaved and a garden appeared. Her name was Sylvia.

She didn't know when her breasts first made themselves known to the world—besides herself—and Little John had reached out, like the homeless for bread, and cupped her breast. *"Son grande, no?"* he laughed, mocking her Spanish. His other hand, feeling left out, had tried to join in. She slapped his hands away and pushed him back.

"Pig. Son of a pig. Cousin of a pig," she screamed in his face, standing her ground. Little John was like red meat with hands, but she hadn't been afraid. She was more afraid of what her papa would've done to her if he had seen. It wouldn't have been her fault. But that didn't matter. All women, except little girls, were sluts until they looked upon the eyes of God. "By God, by God and amen and all that shit," Sylvia laughed to herself as she slapped water over her growing chest.

"Tits," her brother Alex said at dinner that night. He pointed his fork at her, accusing her of thrusting past his manhood. Papa slapped him to the floor. "Sylvia go to your room," was all he said, with mashed potatoes still in his mouth. Mama nodded her head as in sleep. And the garden still grew.

Sylvia splashed water over her pelvis, watching the downy brown hairs sway like tiny seaweeds. She gently touched the growth, as she pictured a farmer would touch his new green sprouts of corn maybe, or wheat, and the scent of the soil would be strong. But then she wondered if wheat was green, or brown as she was brown. Brown down there. Sylvia wondered if fourteen was the age that God turned his eyes away from little girls to make them sluts. Her brother started yelling for her to hurry up. She took one last inspection of her wheat and rose out of the clouds.

The next morning, Little John was waiting on the corner across from St. Gabriel's. He looked as if he had been standing watch all night. Little John had just turned sixteen—he thought he was the shit under God's nails. He went to public school. His hair was greased back and dirty as tar. He flexed meaty lips at her. "Syphilis, how you doin'?" His lips didn't seem to move—he spoke through his teeth. Dirty teeth.

"Are you bothering me, Juanito?" she smiled back at him, flashing her straight, clean teeth. She knew how much he hated being called "Juanito." He was a half-breed like her, except he wanted nobody to know it. Everybody knew it.

"Don' flatter yourself, Syph." She could hear his teeth grinding. "I'm waiting for Niss." He leaned his slouching frame against the lightpost. She saw him as he would look when he got older: big drooping belly a little bigger than his butt. She saw him in his chair watching TV with food in each fist.

"Juanito," his sister Niss called from across the street. Niss was twelve, two years from the wrath and "tits." Sylvia hated that word more than she hated Little John, but she was making herself become used to it. She had a feeling she'd hear it more than she wanted.

Sylvia felt sorry for Niss—but it was more than that. She really liked the small, pudgy girl with the shy smiles; she even smiled at her brother who was so mean to her. She didn't know what she pitied more: Niss for being so nice, or having Little John for a brother. "*Cómo está?*" Sylvia asked.

"*Bueno. Y usted?*" Niss said slowly, correctly. She was trying to help Sylvia with her Spanish.

Sylvia wanted to be able to talk to her Uncle Rudolfo, in Spanish, the next time he came to visit. Unlike her family, Niss's family spoke Spanish openly in the house. Niss's papa was Puerto Rican and her mama was Italian. Niss spoke good Spanish.

"*Cómo, cómo. Bueno, bueno!*" Little John sneered. He turned on his sister. "You shit. We're 'mericans, not spics." He made as if to slap her, and Sylvia edged closer to defend Niss. Little John eyed her for a long moment. His face seemed to suck in on itself in thought. "How do you know you're even half Mex—you might be full," he said quietly. He moved toward her slowly like the Blob did in the movie. She wanted to walk away but she couldn't. "You know what I heard—everyone's heard?" He had her pinned up against the lightpost. One ham fist lightly touched her breast. She wanted to run, puke in his face, scream—but she couldn't. It was just like in those old horror movies, she was stuck.

"You're not half Mex. Maybe all." His hand pressed down harder on her chest, mashing her breast. A fire spread through her, and it was black; a fire that smelled of rotting flesh. His other hand came up. She weakly fended it off—he wasn't really trying that hard. He had his body between her and Niss. Her nipples became diamond points. "We all know your mama's like her mama—a whore."

"Juanito?" Niss's voice sounded scared.

The fire slammed sickness in her brain. She punched him in his chest as hard as she could. He stepped back as if he had never been there, and laughed. "Ask your mama how much she pays for a pound of burger at Romero's?" He turned and pulled Niss the rest of the way to school.

That night in the tub, she scrubbed hard at her breasts. "You're not going to be in there all night, again?" Alex's voice came through the door.

"No." The bruise of an apple rots from the inside out, she thought. She didn't believe Little John—Juanito. She would call him Juanito from now on to prove that he was a big fat liar. She soaked in the clouds of water and tried to forget the fire that burned between her legs. Was she truly thrown out of the garden?

In Spanish class, Stefan had the bluest eyes. He *cómo está*'d better than any other boy. She felt that every time he looked her way, she'd just about spit on herself when she spoke. His eyes passed over her body like searchlights, missing their targets. She smiled hoping to lock those eyes with hers, to look into the sky, but he never seemed to see. She raised her hand as much as possible, *"Yo vivo en Milwaukee,"* and, *"Yo estoy muy bien."*

Niss was in her class also. Since her family spoke Spanish at home, she was allowed into the seventh grade class. Although her brother hated his Hispanic world, Niss seemed happy in it. When Niss spoke the longer sentences, the words, especially the ones heavy with "r's," skipped and rolled off her tongue like well-tossed stones. "*Hablo español muy bueno.*"

Stefan, Sylvia noticed, looked at Niss with a longing she also felt. Stefan, like her, came from a mixed family that didn't speak Spanish at home, and, like her, was trying hard to learn. Sylvia wished she could speak as well as Niss. She would speak just to hear her own voice, and she'd try not to notice (too hard) the looks Stefan would give Niss. In class, when she thought of this, her breasts began to itch.

She was walking Niss home because Little John wasn't there and for the last few days hadn't been there to walk her, when Stefan passed by cradling his books. "*Hola,* Stefan," Niss called.

"*Hola.*" Stefan smiled. He seemed not to look at, or even notice, Sylvia. She seemed to be just a piece of the neighborhood—gray dust.

"Aren't you going to say hi to me, Stefan?" she asked, pushing her chest out until she felt as if she would leap onto his face. He blushed and moved his eyes.

"Sorry, Sylvia. *Hola.*" He dropped his eyes to the ground as if he had weights in his eyeballs.

"Hi, yourself!" she snorted and turned away from him and walked home, feeling both their stares on her back. What's her problem? she could feel both of them ask her back. My problem, she said in her mind, my problem is you—both of you. My problem is that I feel as if I'm sinking into the earth. Don't turn your eyes away from me, Stefan, Mr. Blue Eyes!

She let herself into their flat and called for her mother. Not home. Probably at the butcher's getting burger cheap. "Stop it!" she shouted into the empty hallway.

"Sylv?" Alex called. "Is that you?" He appeared at the top of the stairs. He stood with his hands on his hips, as if blaming her for interrupting the silence of the house. "What the hell are you screaming for?"

"Shut up," she whispered, then stomped into the kitchen. The slippery cleanness of the floor made her want to dump milk onto it—maybe to follow it with cookies, then mash them into the milk with her foot. The stillness of the house, of the kitchen, stopped her. She grabbed an apple and headed to her room to practice her Spanish, to be better than Stefan and Niss. They could all go to hell without a popsicle.

Her mama came into her room as she was just getting the hang of conjugating the verb "to have"—*tener.* "Sylvia," her mama said, weak-eyed, from the doorway, afraid to cross the threshold as if the room would swallow her.

"Mama?" Sylvia yawned. She squared the chair around to face her mama. *"Venga."*

"English!" Mama snapped. "You're not at school. No one speaks that here." Mama's face grew silent and severe. But that moment lasted forever because later Sylvia could remember her face. She could see that once Mama spoke Spanish without effort. "Sylvia, when you bathe I want you to close the door. And, wear loose-fitting clothes . . . "

Mama was stumbling over her lips. "And don't speak that in this house . . . "

"Only when Uncle Rudolfo is here," Sylvia stated.

Her mama's head bobbed, her lips tumbled out "Yes," and she left the room, closing the door quietly behind her.

"I have: *yo tengo,*" Sylvia recited.

"Tú tienes," Niss started.

"You have, informal," Stefan said from behind her. Sylvia spun to him, wanting to be angry for the day before, when he ignored her. "Hi, Sylvia, *cómo está?*" he said, bowing formally. Niss was laughing and Sylvia wanted to be mad, but here she could speak Spanish. Here, behind school, on the swings—not at home in her room. "Good," she smiled back at him, showing her sharp teeth. *"Bueno."*

Stefan sat down on the cement and stared Sylvia in the eye. She swung back and forth lazily, dragging her feet, draw-

ing words in the dirt with her toe. She turned away. Now she
was the shy one. Why? His eyes are blue, she answered to
herself. Blue and different. Niss broke the string of tension that
was forming. "Let's practice irregular verbs. I'll start: *Yo tengo*."

"*Tú tienes*," Stefan said.

"*Nosotros tenemos*," Sylvia finished. "Too easy. Now, to
close: *Yo cierro* . . . "

Sylvia lay in the tub soaking and thinking of Stefan's
blue eyes. The earth heaves up and the sky reaches down.
The firmament is brown—the sky shares blue—together
they become more than heaven. "*Yo cierro:* I close," Sylvia
blew the words over the bubbles. Her breath felt cold on her
chest. "*Tú cierres:* you close. *Nosotros cerramos:* we close."
The mountains rise and God's eye is pierced. The garden
sleeps—the world dies, her mama cries, "Are you going to
drown in there? Hurry!"

Little John walked Niss to the corner everyday, but
avoided Sylvia. She wanted to walk over to him to show
that she wasn't afraid of him and his meat hands, but he
turned away from her before she got up enough nerve. She
asked Niss why Little John was so quiet. "He's in trouble at
school," Niss said, turning her eyes away from Sylvia's. "He
can't cross the street to walk me to school, Papa told him—
it's bad, I think."

Sylvia wanted to say, "Good!" But the sadness on Niss's
face held her back. "Let's go. I'll walk with you everyday—
tell your papa."

Niss smiled—but not really.

Sylvia's Spanish was getting better since she started to
practice more with Stefan and Niss. It became a ritual. Every
day, they would meet after school out on the playground.
Every day, Sylvia and Niss would swing slowly dragging their
toes in the dirt, while Stefan sat below them on the cement-
dirt. *Yo hablo, tú hablas, muy bueno.* Every day the words fell
easier from their tongues, especially Stefan's and Sylvia's,

because Niss could practice at home. Every day they laughed at each other's mistakes—every day Sylvia loved Stefan more, and it hurt.

At home her papa stared at her at dinner with deep sullen eyes. "How's school?" he asked her.

"Good, Papi. I'm doing real good in Spanish class," Sylvia said, pushing her potatoes back and forth on her plate. She heard her mama's intake of breath from across the table. Sylvia smiled.

Papa stared at his fork. "Spanish? How about English? Or math?" he asked, not looking at her or Mama, or Alex who pushed silently away from the table because he'd heard all this before. "I heard Little John was in trouble at his school—something about a sixth-grader . . . "

"Enough," Mama muttered. "Eat."

"*Yo estoy comiendo:* I am eating," Sylvia recited. The table grew still as her words scattered about the dining room.

"Go to your room, Sylvia." Either her mama or papa said it, she didn't hear—she didn't care. She rose with her smile and went to her room.

"You have to understand that your papa doesn't like Spanish spoken in the house," Mama said, later, in her room.

"Why?"

"It's not fair to him," Mama said.

"Why?" Sylvia asked standing in front of Mama—so Mama's eyes had to look at her.

"You don't learn German for him. Do you?"

"Why?" Sylvia said, then, "He doesn't learn Spanish for me."

Mama left the room.

At school neither Sylvia nor Stefan mentioned the rumor of Little John being suspended. Niss seemed to prefer it that way. Sylvia hadn't seen Little John in the neighborhood. They were practicing their Spanish after school when Little John appeared.

He stood a ways off, but Sylvia could still see the bruises on his face. His left eye was puffed out and black. "Was Little John suspended for fighting?" Sylvia whispered.

"No," Niss said, not looking at Sylvia's eyes.

"Niss, Dad wants you home," Little John snarled. Niss's pudgy face pinched up and then she looked at Sylvia.

"*No problemo*, Niss. Tomorrow," Sylvia said, staring at Little John who seemed to be taking an interest in the stones at his feet. Sylvia's whole body became a thing of hate for him.

"*Hasta la vista*," Niss said and left, hanging her head, too, as if the stones had become important.

"Do you still want to practice, Sylvia?" Stefan asked.

"Sure." She watched Niss and Little John disappear into the neighborhood. "Why not?" She wondered at how Niss deserved such a brother as Little John. Sylvia had Alex, and she was glad even for his pesky faults. She turned back to Stefan, "Are you sure you want to practice . . . ?" leaving the words there for him to answer. She moved back and forth from one foot to the next, waiting for him. Boys were so slow sometimes.

"Yes . . . I guess." He stuffed his hands down into his pockets as if he were afraid she would take them and lead him back to the swings where they always studied. Sylvia laughed out loud at the silliness of her thoughts.

"C'mon *ojos de azul*," she said. And she turned her back on him, but not her thoughts or her smile.

"Blue eyes," he said.

"Of course," she laughed.

In the tub that night she thought of boys and men, what the difference was. Her papa looked at her differently now. Why was that? Did he see Mama in her? Her mind, like the steam rising in the tub, wandered to Stefan and his eyes. Then to Little John, then to her papa—back to Stefan. Every time she thought of Little John she wanted to scrub her body, but she didn't know where to start. It was like mosquito bites on your feet. They itched and no matter how much, or where you scratched, it never felt good. She closed her eyes around the steam and let it raise her above thoughts. She touched the earth with her hands. The steam and her hands carried her away. Her hands were harvesting the wheat, and the steam smelled of the fertile soil.

Sylvia wanted to ask Mama if she got hamburger cheaper than everyone else at Romero's. But she didn't. There was a sadness in her mama that she was beginning to notice. She never heard her mama and papa arguing, or yelling, or anything like that. But she felt they did those things to each other from the inside—in bed at night, or at the dinner table—and pulled themselves apart. A look at dinner that followed the passing of the salt. Or at night, maybe, when they turned their backs to each other and coughed or sighed, then listened to the sounds, and then went to sleep, staying out of the other's dreams.

Sylvia wanted dreams. Not dark ones with Little John pawing her as a hungry animal would and being suspended from school. But bright blue dreams where she soared above the earth and exploded with the steam in her baths. She walked to school listening to the things around her for the sounds they made, hoping to distract her thoughts from her mama; her shoes scraping the stones on the sidewalk was the one she decided she liked best. She thought of maybe taking German next year in eighth grade. School was almost over and she could still practice Spanish with Niss's help. Next year she would do both.

In class she caught Stefan looking at her, then he turned away. His eyes found her. Things were different—and Niss was not as eager as before. She still volunteered to speak, but not as much. "*Yo tengo doce años,*" Niss said.

"Sylvia?" The question caught her thinking about other things besides Spanish.

"*Sí?*" she said.

"*Cuántos años tiene?*"

"I have fourteen years," she stammered.

"Think again . . . "

"That was funny, Sylvia," Stefan said. He was on the swing and she was sitting on the cement. Niss was also swinging, laughing. "I have fourteen years . . . "

"Well, at least the verb was right—*tener*—even if it was in English." Sylvia leaned back on her hands, letting her head swing to the side. "How 'bout you Mr. *Ojos?* You didn't do so great today. '*Yo soy enferma,*' you said. What? Are you mental, Stefan?" she laughed.

"That was good," Niss said, then, "I have to go." She dragged her feet, stopping the swing.

"Already?" Stefan said. "We haven't even practiced."

"I know, but I have to go." Niss was looking at the chain-link fence. Little John stood there, sullen, his arms locked tight around himself. Sylvia wanted to tell Little John that they'd take her home, tonight. And every night. Tell him to go where suspended greasy boys go.

Niss looked at her as if Sylvia had spoken out loud. "I have to go—tomorrow we'll just start earlier. *Bueno?*" Niss said.

"*Sí,* I'll stay and practice with Stefan . . . maybe he won't be so sick tomorrow."

"Funny," Stefan said.

"*Mañana,*" Niss said, and walked away. The thought of Little John taking Niss away made Sylvia black inside.

"Sylvia?" Stefan said.

"What?" She turned on him, with the blackness boiling up in her. Stefan was smiling shyly and the blackness almost went away.

Almost went away . . . the steam rose above the bubbles and formed clouds in her mind. The earth flashed in the light and the darkness subsided. The earth rose and settled, as if it, too, had become liquid. She and Stefan had practiced for another half hour when he stood and said he had to go. Why? she asked, they'd just started. No, he had said, and the sky thundered and the earth was drenched in rain. His face became a shadow to her and he fidgeted from one foot to the next. "I have to go," he repeated, as if "go" had become the most important word in the English language. As if "go" became all the letters in the alphabet that she should remember.

"*Yo voy,*" her words echoed in the bathroom. "Close the door, Sylvia," the thunder intruded. He had stood staring down at her and she had smiled; the corners of her mouth had become tight in that smile. Why? she whispered again, and stood up to him. Because, he stammered, I have things I have to do. The wheat swayed in the storm and the mountains shook in the wind. He was ready to fly—to grab the wind and let it carry him away. "Dammit, I said close that door!" She had moved closer to him, and his feet stopped moving. He leaned closer to her as if he wanted something. Something, she thought. His eyes pierced her and she knew. She moved closer, almost touching him with her breasts—she knew.

He was hesitant. But she knew. Would you like to touch? she asked him and the mountains settled. What? he had said. What? The wind swirled and the sky moved away. No, no, he said. And then the blackness went away. He stumbled back away from her, his face knowing and not knowing why, and she was wrong. The earth settled and the garden was gone. "Sylvia," Mama stood at the open door. "Did you hear me?"

The thunder was off in the distance and the clouds dissipated. The wheat swayed gently, waiting for harvest, and heaven abandoned earth. Sylvia smiled in the steam, "*Cierra la puerta, Mama . . .* " The door closed.

Roundabout

"Jillian is bordering on obstinacy," she heard her mother say once to her father. Earholes are for keyholes, she thought then in response, and now, too, she felt the same. All the secrets of the world were there; they were ear-level when you're on your knees, and could also accommodate the eye; babies were conceived there, and Santa Claus died there along with the Easter Bunny; her brother smoked pot and her Uncle Jim was heard to be gay there—she had thought him to be real happy, but knows different; her grades were discussed and punishment was conspired there; her best friend's parents' divorce was there, waiting, like hers was, to be heard later.

Her father grunted at everything her mother said, and she wondered if they ever talked at all to each other. She couldn't seem to remember. He believed he was a True Marxist who was kidnapped as a child and brought to the US. He knew this, he told the family every holiday, because he was always poor. And to conclude, he'd say the poor are not supposed to get poorer—they're just poor.

Capitalism was the heaviest yoke to bear, he'd pound the table with his bearlike fists, spitting, during Christmas dinner, or Easter, and even Thanksgiving. Only in America can you become poorer. At least in the old country you

knew what you were and accepted it. Her father had been
born in Detroit.

She and her brother Sammy, a year older—Sammy
with the long gold hair like hers—ignored their father and
his tirades as if they were part of what they knew the holidays to be. Her brother was a proclaimed atheist and left
home when he was seventeen to join the army, then died
later in a war, in some gulf, in some country that no one but
the government cared about, leaving only a letter to her sa
ing that he was reconsidering his position on religion.

Jillian considered herself an antagonistic agnostic—
two words that sounded and felt comfortable when she
decided on them. She felt, when *she* turned seventeen, that
she needed a designation of some kind as Sammy did, and
Marxism wasn't to her liking. Jillian felt she was antagonistic to everything—especially, now, second mortgages and
second marriages. At twenty-three she married John and
moved to Tucson with him. As far as possible from her parents. John built her a house her father wouldn't have been
proud of (if he had ever been to it) and placed her and her
existence there among keyholes. She left everything behind,
not the least of which was Sammy's last letter, which she'd
framed and hung in her room at home the day she got married to John. It was still there.

She was at the keyhole while her husband was on the
phone with his banker friend. Well, I would take a second
and use it to pay for the divorce . . . I'll come out ahead in
the long run. Then—right, right. Hey, I'm not cold . . . of
course I'll pay for her lawyer too. Your cousin? Fine.

When she heard *the divorce*, it pushed her ear and body
from the keyhole so that she landed on her butt. The soft
whump, as if air was escaping from her skin, made her husband pause in his conversation. She stared at the solid wood
of the door, expecting to see John's pointed face accusing

her, but he continued as if he hadn't heard—safe in the thought that he was above keyholes and wives.

Her mother was a marcher and parader of beliefs. Religion was the beat and palm that choreographed her steps: Catholicism pulled her in by her black beaded rosary, then pushed her back out to march and parade. Her mother didn't wave fire and brimstone from a broom, or spoon, but exhibited a persistent belief throughout the holidays, more so on Christmas and Easter. Birth and death. At Christmas her mother put a shine on her face that reflected the Christmas tree star, the elaborate table setting with Jesus in the manger, and her father's brooding face. On Easter her mother hid boiled eggs all over the house. All year, rotten, colored eggs would pop up in the strangest places.

Jillian and John had been married three years, child-less, before she noticed the change in his face. It happened when they decided to fly to Milwaukee to visit for Christmas. At first it seemed John was eager to please her—what were a few bucks? He could take off from the broker-age firm for two weeks. They planned, packed, boarded the plane, and were off.

Christmastime was when her father's Marxist doppel-ganger came to life. It seemed to rub off on John, because the expenses were totaled: plane tickets, rental car, and the Christmas gifts they'd bought for her parents. John was still eager to visit, but after being with her father for a day, he seemed less so, and it showed. When they all kissed and sat down to Christmas dinner, her mother said a prayer for the soul of her brother, a prayer for Jillian finally remembering to visit them—and God, where were the grandchildren? The star and silverware reflected from her mother's face as she prayed. Her father brooded. She looked at John and he was smiling serenely.

They had left her parents' home a week earlier than planned, John claiming important, forgotten business. He said he was sorry, and that he would make it up to her—somehow. Next year, he promised as he handed over the rental car keys to the cherub-faced girl behind the counter. Jillian and John smiled politely—her smile was forced. The plane vibrated beneath Jillian as she scanned the terminal window for her mother and father. She caught a glimpse of their faces as the plane taxied away. She frantically waved at the reflections in the smoky glass—her mother, on the road to God, and her father, one foot in the poor house—waved back.

The flight home was quiet. I'm tired and need some sleep, he yawned, patting her hand, I need my strength. The plane lifted over Milwaukee and the clouds swallowed up the plane. Wake me before we land, Jillian? She nodded to the window, sure.

She occupied herself with the flight magazines from the seat pocket in front of her. She looked at the pictures only, too tired for the words. After about ten minutes she glanced at John. His eyes fluttered for a second, then lay still. She returned to her pictures, glancing every so often to see if he was really sleeping—and each time his eyes fluttered. Glance, flutter. Glance, flutter. He's watching me, she thought. He pretends to sleep so he doesn't have to talk to me. Well, two can play that. She put the magazine away and tilted her seat back farther than his. She watched him the rest of the way home.

She watched him the rest of the year, too, unsure of his face. She noticed his nose was a little more pointed than she ever thought. And his eyes were much too close together. But she gave in to the eyes because they matched his one eyebrow, stretched across his forehead like an upside-down grin that connected his ears. His chin was much more fierce than before, she knew it—she knew it! During dinner he chewed each mouthful twenty-three times, and cleared his throat constantly. Plus, he grunted between bites. His smiles, his voice, eyes, ears (now red), and chin pointed and pierced her. Money was all that concerned him, and she was his damn moth floating around his flame. His existence. He hated her and she knew it.

Maybe he'd always hated her and she only just began to notice it, she thought. Her days were spent at her hobbies, as John called them—she volunteered for everything: hospitals, shelters, Native American causes. Anything that came along. You're from Milwaukee, not Tennessee, John said. She never got the connection. She just knew he hated her.

Jillian called her mother to ask how she handled Father all these years. Jillian, her mother gasped, twice in one whole year you're speaking to me. Praise God. Her voice couldn't find itself in the words she wanted to say. Instead, she stayed with the banal stuff that seemed commonplace between her and her parents—just like her mother never calling her Jilly. Mother how have you been? How's Father? Fine, fine. Good-bye Mother. Calling her mother only brought up the memory of her brother Sammy—only he called her Jilly. She thought of his picture, alone, in her room. He'd abandoned her when he left home. She hated him for it.

The year before he left her, he started teaching her how to sail. Almost every day, that last summer, when the weather permitted, he took her sailing in the boat he had scrounged, it seemed, his whole life to buy. She went with him, not really caring to learn. She wanted only to be out alone, away from her parents, with Sammy. The two of them, twins, people sometimes thought, she the shy one and Sammy the grinning one, would settle into the boat with only nods to each other that said, yes, we are here. And that *here* was all that mattered to Jillian. But he had betrayed her by going away. She had thought that *here* mattered just as much to him.

We're children of fucked-up parents, Jilly, he told her when they were on Lake Michigan during one of his attempts at letting her sail. He said it without much inflection, which surprised her, as one might say, I think it's going to rain today—and after he said it, it rained.

The lake became rough and Sammy began shouting orders on how to tack in the wind, changing directions abruptly to keep up with the slashing gusts that pushed her one way, and then slapped her back the other. She was getting sick. The waves had been so beautiful when they left the marina. They were far from shore, and the wind picked up to hurricane force, always changing its mind as to which way it wanted to buffet them. Sammy laughed, Hurricane? This isn't shit, Jilly. Sammy's hair whipped around his face, sweeping the large grin he wore as if there were strings attached to his scalp and the wind was the puppeteer.

Then he suddenly yelled, Come about! And she ducked barely in time—the boom just missing her. Sammy stared at her hard, pushing her roughly out of the way, and took over. She was numb as Sammy shortened the sail and brought them back to the marina; she sat there like a statue made of ice. But not because Sammy berated her. No, because he yelled, Stupid bitch! How many times do I have to tell you to watch out for the boom . . . took your damn head off . . . never be a sailor . . . That was the first time he had ever called her a bitch—and it was the last.

But Sammy didn't tell her that day on the lake about the army—that day he sentenced her to the condition of their family and called her a bitch. No, and he didn't tell when he was sneaking downtown to take his physical. Her father never mentioned it, either. It had dawned on her that her father must've known, he had to sign because Sammy was underage. Instead, Sammy told her after he was already gone—in a letter that claimed his religious beliefs were changing.

The army had the stamp of her father's approval. The only sane institution in this insane society, he'd said, waving his bear fists. That was the first time she'd seen her father smile while he brooded. She was confused with this image until the Government men came and said they were so sorry, and then, she saw her own face in the mirror—the same face as her father's, a brooding smile.

She decided that she still didn't forgive Sammy when she hung up the phone from talking to her mother, and didn't have plans to do so in the near future.

Into the new year she gave up her *hobbies* and concentrated on creating a spotless home and warm meals. Even when John didn't come home for dinner, she had a steaming plate of something at his place. She leaned on her hands, trying to imagine what John's face had looked like before they went to visit her parents. No matter how hard she tried, the only image she could conjure up was a woodpecker head. An angry woodpecker without a tree to peck. And when John was there, he wasn't, really. He was off in some forest pounding other trees. She might as well be wood, Jillian thought, as she watched him chew and chew.

She called her mother back right after she heard the phone conversation between John and his banker friend. She asked her mother if she and Father had ever discussed divorce. Divorce? her mother said. It's a sin. A sin, dear. She could picture a large yawn. Divorce? her father's voice sounded from a distance. Capitalistic—fantastic. Only in America. A sin, a sin, her mother kept rattling like old dishes. Then her voice became cheery, Remember Mike and Cindi? Well they're having a baby . . . Good-bye, Mother. Jillian hung up.

She decided the best thing to do was confront John about their impending divorce. Catch him off guard. Tell him she would refuse a second mortgage. No lawyers—no kickbacks to friends on the phone. They'd just file together. She didn't care what she did after, she'd say. But she knew one thing, she wasn't going back to her parents. She wondered if twenty-six was too old for the army.

John came home when he pleased and left the same way without so much as a How are you, dear? She kept up the pretense of cleaning and meals. At the end of May she tried a different approach.

How are you? she asked him one night. Fine, he answered, chewing his food. I was thinking of getting a job, Jillian said, rolling stray peas with her fork, not looking up from her plate. That stopped John and his chewing. Haw, he said. What are you going to do? What can you do? His fingers were tearing apart a slice of bread into tiny pieces. Really, Jillian, what do you want to do? He returned to his food. I don't know, she replied. I just know I can do something. Just as long it doesn't cost us any more money—do what you want, John said, and went pecking away.

The next day Jillian packed a suitcase and caught the first flight to Milwaukee. She left a note for John telling him she had to go visit her parents, and for him not to worry, and she'd call him. She never mentioned the divorce then, nor did she say when she was coming back.

Jillian, Jillian, her mother gasped. Twice. What's wrong? Are you sick? Her mother poured her a cup of coffee. I know—you're pregnant. My dear, are you sure this is smart? But I thought you wanted grandchildren, Mother? No, no. Much too messy. Diapers. Always spitting up. Her mother spoke rapidly, motioning around the kitchen, as if reminding her of the places Jillian messed up when she was a baby.

What? A baby? Who's having a baby? Jillian? her father said, coming into the kitchen. No, Father, I'm not pregnant. I just came to visit—that's all, Jillian said, blowing on her hot coffee. She hated coffee. I should hope not! My God, do you know what bringing a child into this world entails? Money. Capitalistic values imposed upon . . . Stop! Father, I'm not pregnant, Jillian breathed into her coffee cup. She held it to her chin, letting the aroma wash over her face. Anyway, her mother picked up where her father left off,

Jillian is here—thank God. And honey? You shouldn't drink coffee when you're pregnant. Jillian hated coffee and her mother.

Jillian didn't call John that first night, or the second either. She wanted him to call her to ask her why she'd left—but he didn't. Then it became a matter of her just staying away from home and her parents. She spent most of her time down by the lakeshore, watching owners christen their sailboats for the new season. The sizes of the boats amazed her. The boat that Sammy took her out on was a bathtub toy compared to the ones she watched. The long-bed semi would drive in, maneuvering backwards to the lake, slowly, then they'd off-load the boats to majestically bob like crowns in the water. The owners would mount the decks and proudly ride as the marina personnel guided them to their new berths.

She was hanging around so much at the marina that she became part of the scenery there. A "sea dog," as the old man called himself, took up the task of being her friend. They were quite the pair: he was short and walked bow-legged where she was long of leg and walked gingerly as if she was afraid to offend the ground; his hair was sparse and gray on top and seemed to stand on end in the wind like a wild man's—hers was soft and moved about her face, giving her an aspect of melancholy.

She would smile absently, thinking of Sammy, while the seadog told stories about his voyages on the Great Lakes. She nodded appropriately, and kept up the pretense of listening lest she offend him. She thought of it as the same as feeding the sea gulls. People fed them so they didn't have to be alone—Jillian had a sea dog.

John called at the end of her first week at her parents'. Jillian? Yes, John, she sighed, not surprised that he called. Hmm, I can't find the important papers, he said. What important papers? Jillian yawned into the phone. You know, the ones for the mortgage and stuff. He sounded impatient. Jillian switched the receiver to her other ear. They're in the strongbox, where they always are. His voice became small, oh. Um, where would that be? On the top shelf in our closet, she said. Oh, he said. And John? Yes? I'm doing fine. Oh, he said again. Don't you wonder when I'll be home? she said. No. I mean, I suppose when you're done doing whatever it is you're doing. Bye, John. Jillian hung up.

Where do you go all day? her mother asked her the next morning. Jillian was drinking a cup of coffee—she decided she would like it. I go to the marina. I'm taking sailing lessons. Sailing lessons? Since when? You don't sail. Sailing? Her father came into the kitchen. Who's sailing? Jillian is, her mother rolled her eyes at her father. Sailing? Do you know how much that costs? Sailing, hmm. Jillian blew over her coffee, actually, it's my first lesson . . . and it's free. Don't you get seasick, dear? her mother said. Sailing, free? Fantastic! her father put in. Jillian decided she was definitely liking coffee.

Now, when the wind shifts you have to be ready for it, the old sea dog was telling her. His hands were flying in front of him as he spoke, trying to imitate with his fingers the directions of the wind. And when beginning to tack you have to be ready for the switch—watch the boom, or it'll take 'er head off. Jillian nodded, her hair gently flitting around her face in the wind. The lake was calm. The sky was blue. A good day for sailing. She held the tiller under her arm, comfortably, and smiled absently to the old man's instructions as if she heard every word.

The gentle rhythm of gliding over the waves lulled her into the past with Sammy. She could feel those times out on the lake with just Sammy and the waves. The old man was explaining to her how, when he gave the word, she was to turn into the wind and come about watching, of course, for the boom. Those days seemed to flow like the water when Sammy and she were out sailing—her sitting in the front of the boat, trailing her fingers in the foam and wishing they never had to go back. Sammy at the tiller whistling "Blow the Man Down." There were no marriages in the waves, or parents, or even the thought of a second mortgage. It was just the wind and the feeling of flying through the water.

The old man was lost in his own story, and her head bobbed with a life of its own to show her interest. There were no thoughts of dying in a war somewhere—just Sammy and the wind.

Jillian must've turned the tiller in her remembering because the old man's voice fluttered to a stop, then roared, Come about! Jillian was past hearing, and ducked long before the boom got near her. She didn't even hear the old man berate her for not warning him that she was going to tack—but she heard him, or Sammy, say what a fine maneuver it was. Just like a seasoned sailor. She smiled, tasting on her lips the water that was not unlike salt.

The Dog God

I remember him, Bird. I was ten and that summer my dog, Rigby, died, I believed in his magic—or believed he had it. I was sitting by the trestle, throwing stones into the slough. He was in the marsh running from mud clump to mud clump, dodging the patches of water. He was tan and ten, also. I remember how he appeared out of the sun as a shadow, startling me for a moment. He was running without a shirt and with his arms outstretched among the duck nests. He was squawking. Standing in front of me like a muddied duck, he said his name was Guermo. I said, "No, you're a bird."

I sat and watched him as the purple martins alighted from out of nowhere on his arms for a second, and then disappeared into the blue sky like ghosts. His squawking echoed the cries of the mother ducks trying to protect their young from this strange human bird. His constant weaving among the mud clumps and nests finally quieted them down as if they accepted his strangeness as one of their own. "See," he said, returning to me, sitting with his chocolate legs dangling next to mine over the dark water of the slough. "I have magic."

"Hmm . . . " I said.

"Yes," he continued, as if I didn't doubt him. "I can talk to the birds in their own language and they take me as one of their own." He raised an arm against the blue cloudless sky and a martin was magically there, then gone. I blinked against the shadow his arm made against the sky. "And that's not all. In my family we talk and pray to the Mother, and She listens." I knew then that he was Indio and Mexican. My mama sometimes talked that way.

"I'm Marie," I said, throwing stones into the mud. "My papa works at the foundry. We just moved here from Texas."

"Uhmm . . . same here. Mi papi grew up in Neenah, but moved away . . . we've been here a year. I am trying to make this my place," he said and stood, waving his arm over the marsh, including Lake Butte de Mors—including the paper mills that hugged the shores in the distance, pouring out their garbage into the lake. "Look," he shouted at the slickness of oils that hugged the edges of the marsh mud. "I will clean this up."

I nodded my head. "I saw the same thing in Texas, where we used to live."

He sat back down and picked up a rock, "Yes, me too."

Like most of the families in our neighborhood, we were new. My father worked in the foundry, a steel mill that turned father and the neighborhood into a dark hazy cloud of smoke. A sign on top of the lone smoke stack said 99 percent steam, but we knew better. Most of us kids were half-breeds, Mexican and Polish, or German, and some full-bloods like Guermo's family, who didn't even speak English. My mama barely spoke English, but we all got by, somehow.

It all started when Rigby had been getting into the garbage—so Papa started to keep her outside. There was an old kennel built along the garage with a doorway cut in the side, so Rigby could sleep in shelter. "See," Papa assured me, "she'll be all right—snug as a bug." He helped me fix up a place for her to sleep with old blankets, ones Mama said weren't old enough for a dog. mama didn't think any dog was worth anything. "Your mama came from a poor family," Papa explained, "and dogs and cats weren't . . . " he searched for the right way to tell me, as he always did, "a luxury they could afford. Do you understand?"

He was on his knees, eye-level with me, as he always was when he talked to me. My father was a big man, strong like the metal he worked with for sometimes sixty hours a week. I didn't see my father, in summer, for a whole week. In the summers, when the foundry was really busy, he worked from sunup to past my bedtime. And the only times I remember seeing him—really seeing him without all that black soot on him—were on Sundays.

Rigby took to her new home with a whine when she realized she was no longer welcome in the house at night. I wanted to sleep with her that first night to keep her company, but that's where Mama drew the line. "First my good blankets, now you, too? No, it's just a dog!" I went to bed listening to Rigby cry. Rigby eventually accepted her lot as long as she didn't have to be in the kennel during the day. I took her back by the marsh with me to run. She loved the tall marsh grass and made the ducks nervous though she never intruded on them. Bird-boy was always there, and Tom-Tom, another "half-breed migrant" as the other kids liked to tease us, though you could tell they were only repeating what they had heard and didn't really put their hearts into it. We three became inseparable: Bird, with his long chocolate body, and Tom-Tom and me, the olive-skin twins, as Bird called us. It was our world alone by the tracks and marsh, watching Bird cure the world. We never doubted.

We had heard about the Dog God from the other kids who had lived in the town for their whole lives. He was an ancient old man of indiscriminate ancestry who plied the country roads picking up junk and wounded animals. He was said to be a saint by some and a sorcerer by others, depending on who told the story. Bird claimed he was a saint who saved animals, other kids said their parents took their pets to him to be "put away" so they didn't have to pay the thirty dollars the Humane Society charged. We believed Bird. Or I did until my father took Rigby there.

Rigby became sick in July and at first we thought it was because of the garbage she was getting into. Then we thought of worms. It was subtle at first, she wouldn't eat even when I sneaked her a piece of baloney—her and my favorite. She was fine for a while then, eating again but not as much. "Marie," my father woke me early one morning before he went to work. I knew it was important for him to do that. "Marie, does Rigby eat the plants when you kids play by the marsh? Flowers, grass?" I was groggy and barely understood what he was saying—he repeated himself again and I caught "eat . . . things . . . marsh?"

"No," I shook my head, aware that my father was really concerned. "I don't think so, Papa. Is she really sick?" He hesitated, then said, "I don't know . . . maybe. Do me a favor and watch her when you're by the lake, okay?"

"Do you think Rigby should go? I mean if she's sick . . . "

"No, take her. She loves it. Just keep two eyes on her." He kissed my forehead and moved away. I thought, Bird can cure her!

By the beginning of August, Rigby was moved back in the house at night. She lay quietly on the floor at the end of my bed sleeping—too tired to even go to the marsh and lake. Bird did dances on the mud clumps for her, shaking pebbles into the muddy water. He told me it would take time, but he said honestly he didn't know if he could cure what he didn't see. "I can see this." He pointed at the growing oily buildup along the shore and mud. "But . . . "

I was starting to believe Bird wasn't any different than me or Tom-Tom, just maybe sadder. He did all his squawking and jumping around and the lake continued to get uglier day by day.

By the end of August, Papa took Rigby to the vet, taking a couple hours off from work against Mama's protests of money wasted, and came back without her. It was in the garage, he said, and it had been all the time. Rigby had gotten into some poison. "Poison?" I said quietly, too shocked to even cry. "What? How? Where is she, Papa?"

Papa held his dirty hands in front of him, not even able to have washed them yet. "I took her to be put to sleep." He stared at me, daring me, supplicating me—now that I look back—not to ask where. Mama started to put in again about spending the money, but he cut her off with a solid cutting movement of his dark hand—then I knew. My father had taken her to the Dog God. To save money? To save her? With a look at Mama, I knew it was to save money. Maybe the vet could've saved her but Papa couldn't, or wouldn't, spend the money.

"*Hija*," Mama said, coming to me. "I'm sorry, *lo siento mucho*, but we cannot afford . . . " I left them there, in their final poses, before I walked out the door, never again to feel the same about them, especially my father. "Forever," the screen door closed shut with a slam, "Different," my tennis shoes whispered as I hurried across the street to the railroad tracks to find Bird and Tom-Tom.

I explained to them what happened and I could see something unsure in Bird. He had failed me, and even at that age I instinctively played on it. "I need to go to the Dog God's farm," I said looking directly at Bird—he knew the way.

"It's five miles, out of town," Tom-Tom complained. "It's afternoon already. We won't be back until after dark."

"We can take the tracks to Harrison Street, then to County 'A.' It will be shorter . . . but it is still two miles from town," Bird said, then pushing at Tom-Tom. "Not five miles, stupid!"

"Stop," I said. "We must go, now." I saw the hesitation in Bird's face, but I knew he would go—even against a whippin', but I wasn't so sure about Tom-Tom, he was scared of his father.

But it was already decided, those many years ago, we would all go find out what the Dog God was all about. I wanted Rigby back . . . I wanted, I guess, to feel that special way I felt about my papa doing the impossible, even against Mama's wishes.

We started right away, all but me thinking of punishment—mine was already happening. There was nothing more my parents could do to me. "Tell us more about this Dog God," Tom-Tom sighed, accepting his fate full-face.

"Atta boy," I whispered behind them, not knowing or caring if they heard or not.

"Well, mi papi says that he is old even when mi papi is young. This old man who collects junk like tires, hubcaps, metal, animals—alive or dead from the roadside. 'As long as there has been roads,' Papi says, 'there has been this *viejo.*'"

Bird looked at both of us—we shook our heads yes, we understood the word. "Mi papi was shocked to hear that this man still existed when we came here. I don't know math too well, so I don't even know how old he could be.

"Anyway, this old man has this reputation of nobody hardly seeing him, or if they do, they don't agree on what he looks like." We made it to Harrison Street and headed north to the end of town and County Trunk "A." "Some say his face turns the animals he finds alive to stone to end their suffering, others say he just," Bird stopped, looked at me. "You know. Anyway, the older half-breed Indios like my mama say that they are turned to stone, then taken to his farm to be healed by the heaven he has captured behind his gates. There, he lets them go and they run and live like in the Garden—happy, forever," Bird laughed all of a sudden at the way he told the story, just like an adult trying to scare children with religion.

"Anyway," Bird said, holding out his arms as if signaling their approach to the Devil's Throat, "the other stories are too scary to think of just right now, *verdad?*"

"*Sí!*" Tom-Tom and I nodded.

I had only been through the small stretch of road called Devil's Throat, mostly by the older kids, in our car. It swung uphill past the cemetery like a snake, as if swallowing itself in dark greenness. It was about suppertime, we judged, when we passed through it. "No big deal," Tom-Tom said, and we all laughed. "Except comin' back, no?" He laughed alone.

"We'll be back way before dark," Bird said. "It is only about a mile down the road."

We quickly passed the cemetery and left the shadowed road behind. The afternoon was cooler than usual, probably because of the lateness of the season and because we were all usually home eating supper by now. The coolness reminded me that we had to hurry. My papa would know where we all took off to, once it was known all of us were late for supper. I just bet on the fact that he would go back to work to make up for the precious time and money he wasted that day. I took the lead, setting the pace in front of Bird. He caught up to me, not wanting to relinquish his role as leader of our expedition, and passed by, setting an even faster pace that neither Tom-Tom nor I was going to argue with. We reached and passed County Trunk "S" and continued down our road. We had been walking more than a mile. "Did we pass it?" Tom-Tom blew out.

"No," Bird said, not showing any doubt. "There," he pointed, "that dirt road is the one Papi pointed out to me as his road." We followed his finger and up ahead of us about fifty yards was the entrance to the Dog God's farm. Where he pointed was also the beginning of a vast stretch of woods that ran down County "A" on one side for as far as we could see. At the edge of the woods was the driveway, just covered enough by the woods that it obscured the view of the farm from the road. On this side of the farm we could see rows of late feed-corn.

"He farms?" I asked. "You didn't say if he farmed. This can't be his place."

"Sí, he don't have to farm. It might be sold land already, or some share cropper . . . like in Texas, no?"

"Yes," I said not wanting to believe we were there. I was afraid and didn't want to really see Rigby dead. My Papa a traitor. My Mama right. Tom-Tom was afraid, but not of what lay ahead, it was his own behind he was worrying about.

"Let's go and . . . " he said, stomping on ahead of us. He got to the driveway then turned back on me. "What're we supposed to be doing? Huh?"

Bird and I reached him and saw what was behind him, a sign. "Goddard's farm," it started. I wanted Bird to do some kind of magic, to make Rigby come out alive; I wanted everything to be like it was when the summer started. I didn't want fall, or school. To wear dresses, and hard shoes. My mother making me brush and then her braiding my hair. My papa leaving and coming while it was still dark. His coughing and black coming out on his hankie. I didn't want to be able to read English at that moment, something I was so proud of. The sign said, "Goddard's farm, pets taken care of—fifteen dollars—cheap!" The sign was the only thing that looked new on that stretch of road. "Let's go," I said, and I started to walk back to home and what was waiting for me there.

An Absence of Roses

Roses were my grandmother's favorite. She gave my mother a slip from a bush she had brought over from Poland when she was a girl. My grandmother planted it in our backyard before I was born and helped it grow, without help from my mother, strong and full—until I was ten. Grandma lived in the same town we did, about three miles away—it was like a second home to us. When we visited her during the spring and summer, she would be working in her garden, pruning and weeding her various plants: tomatoes, beans, peas. And, she would always come in with a fresh-cut rose from her own bush, making it the centerpiece of the kitchen table. Then she'd tell stories to my brother Paul and me.

And as we got older, her stories seemed to become harsher. It was as if time, hers and ours, was meeting on some middle ground. A ground that as I became older and older, was more familiar, but only as I passed over it in hindsight. It was into those stories my brother and I grew, unaware of the changes from the happy times on her farm to the time when that life was taken from her. We accepted the stories as we accepted her slower movements when the seasons were changing and she couldn't grow things; she spent the idle hours telling us these stories.

It was 1977 and I was seventeen and had come over alone to shovel snow for Grandma on a Saturday morning, a ritual my brother and I shared every winter since we were old enough to lift a shovel. I put my back into it and sweated. Afterwards, she heated up some stuffed cabbage and warmed some cider she had made herself. Paul was older than I, and was too caught up in his own stuff to worry about Grandma. I was angry at him, and I told her so, because it had only been a year since Grandma took him and my mother to Poland. I had wanted to go with Grandma; it was I who dreamed of the places that came through her in stories—not Paul, or my mother. Or so, at least, I believed.

She was aware of the change in my brother, but it didn't seem to concern her. "Ah, Rafel, always they come back. You kids." She winked and then said something in Polish and laughed. "Plus, I have so many grandchilds . . . he'll come back when he is older."

I smiled as I sipped the warm cider. "You talk as if he's gone away. He'll be here to shovel next time," I said, watching her move around the kitchen.

She was always doing something, my grandmother, always circling around cleaning this, straightening that, cooking. "Sit," I said patting the table next to me. She had on her housecoat and slippers still. She stopped for a moment as if to settle into a time frame and pulled her housecoat close to herself.

"It's getting late, and I am not even dressed . . . "

"C'mon, Grandma, sit."

She pointed a finger at me as she sat, and I knew it was time. "You . . . you grinner." She waved the finger in my face. "You kids are lucky. Listen.

"I am sixteen and I am taking the clothes off the line. It is August and it already doesn't get too warm until afternoon. But the clothes still dry in the cold wind. Our yard isn't like it is here, it is dirt and dust all around. I remember hating to sweep the dirt dust ground. We didn't have floors like you kids do, here—we had dirt for our floors. And there is twelve of us living in a small house, half the size of mine here. My job every morning is to do the wash, hang it, and sweep the dust. I would get water from the well and sprinkle it on the floor to . . . to—quiet it down? Anyway, I am taking the wash in and the day is cool. Already I can feel the winter coming and it is only August!

"I can see the well and stone barn, because stone doesn't burn, and by our wood cow-fence is standing this man. I never see him before, so I watch him as I pull and fold the clothes, pretending I am not looking. He stands there and stares at me—a big man. Pig, I think. I hear the swine in the pen and laugh to myself, almost dumping the clothes on the line. I will have to wash them all over again myself, and maybe even get a whipping from my mama—there is too much to do already.

"My nine brothers are all off in the fields with my papa getting in the wheat before it dies from the cold. By August it is our third harvest. Ah, summers are so hard there. I can see them far away, too far, if this man wants trouble. Everyone has been scared since the Germans are just done making trouble . . . what do you call it? Oh, after the big war I. So I just watch this man, who's leaning on our fence and watching me. Only his face and hands are bare—he is too far for me to see clear, but he must be a swine, I think.

"I fold the last towel and stuff it into the basket. I pick up this big, full basket, what is almost too heavy for me, but I am strong."

She stopped there as if she needed to keep moving in the present, not to let her stories catch up. She went to the sink, holding the front of her housecoat as if she could feel that chill August, hanging clothes again. I think I realized then that my grandmother was once a beautiful woman. I had seen pictures of her when I was younger, but I couldn't connect the beautiful girl with my grandmother until that moment. My grandmother had long brown hair and her eyes

were metallic—glistening in the black and white photo-
graph. From the faucet she poured herself a glass of water, all
with one hand, never releasing her housecoat.

I finished my cider and sat back watching Grandma
move around the kitchen again as if making sure things
hadn't moved, touching her toaster, Mister Coffee, refrigerator, lightly touching her stove, as if to remind herself those
things were real. She sat back down and coughed. She
hunched over her glass, holding it with both hands for the
coolness. "You kids need to see both sides."

I didn't answer her. I nodded, looking into my empty
mug, and she went on.

"That man scares me and I don't know why. I don't
scare easy, being the only sister with all those brothers. I pull
up that heavy basket and rest it on my hip. Keeping that
man in one eye, I go to the door. '*Mamushka!*' I yell, kicking
the door." My grandma kicked me under the table and I
almost laughed out loud, but I didn't want to break her train
of thought. "'Open the door, *prosze?* *Di me spokojne,*' Mama
calls from inside, pulling the door open. I almost fall inside
and spill those clothes again, on our dirt floor. 'Alicia,'
Mama yells, helping me set them down. 'Girl,' she always
says, 'you are going to be the death of me.'

"'Sorry, Mama, there's a strange man by the cow fence,'
I point out the one back window we have.

"'Ay?' She walks over and pulls the curtain back and I
can see the fence but no one is there. The sun is just making
it to the top of the day and soon my papa and brothers will
come from the fields for food. Mama just looks at me and I
know I will watch out. 'We have to make food!' Mama says.

"My brother Jusef, he is two years younger, the only one
who live after the big war II, comes in the house first followed by Vwadik, then Stacik, the youngest; they eat first
because they will feed the plow horses while the other older
men eat, no time to waste. *Ach!* Mama is always yelling at

my younger brothers who are so stupid not to take the mud boots off and put on shoes before they come in—boys, ah, they give my mama white hair." Grandma stopped and looked at me, on the verge of remembering something else. She took a swallow of her water, and set the glass to stand alone on the table.

Her fingers were strong from working in the garden, the house, from raising eight of her own children—without a husband's help. My grandfather died when my mother was thirteen, and this was all in Grandma's fingers. "Boys!" she said, shaking her head. Then she fell silent, letting her chin rest on her breast bone, and stared into her glass.

□ ○ □

When I was ten, I was fascinated with the thorns on the rose bush. The bush was ten feet from our back door, and in the spring we navigated a precarious peace with the bees to the door. In the summer, passing too close tore clothes and scratched skin. My mother was always reminding me when I went outside to stay clear of that damn bush. "You come in with another rip or bloody scratch, and I'll pull that damn bush out with my teeth. I told Grandma that bush would be too close to the door," she'd say. I would snap off a thorn as big as my pinky and attach it to the end of a stick with black electrical tape. Using it as a spear, I hunted wild tigers in our small backyard, or speared the rotting apples that fell from our tree.

My brother, for some reason, never tangled with the bush. He'd twist the skin on my arms, giving me "snake bites," and say, "Ma pulls out that damn bush, and I'll tell Grandma it was 'cause you're so stupid." He was always threatening to tell Grandma on me about something because one day Grandma declared that she and our mother were going to go back to Poland one day to see her *matka*, before she died, and might take one of us kids along. I wanted to go just as bad as my brother did. I tried to stay clear of that bush for a while, and stuck to falling out of our apple tree. But I always came back to that bush.

I never got along with the things growing in our yard. Even when I cut our small patch of grass, the lawn mower would find the only rock or stick and spit it back at me, cutting me on the arms or legs. My mother would clean me up and I could see her thinking about that bush. If only she would've realized it was everything in the yard that hated me. She held me firmly with one big hand, and cleaned my wound, "Stay away from that bush."

My mother was an imposing woman—big-boned. She was the third youngest behind five brothers of her own and she was strong. Once, I called my brother a bastard, and my mother heard. She grabbed me by the arm and held me, not hurting, but almost, and said, "One time I called my brother Joe a bastard—he spit water on my Sunday dress. I was so mad. Anyway, Grandma heard. I never was beaten so hard in my life. She held this belt that was my dad's, and let it dangle like this," she shook her arm down as if she held a whip, "and beat me. Grandma took me literally—I never saw her so mad." Still, I never thought my mother would pull that damn bush out—or make my dad do it. Because, after all, the bush had come all the way over from Poland, as Grandma told us.

That summer when I was ten, my brother and I were playing catch in the backyard and the ball ended up in the middle of the bush. I reached in to pull out the ball. I was balancing on one foot, gingerly trying to not catch myself on the thorns while my brother, behind, taunted me. "C'mon Rafel, you wimp, get it." I lost my balance and fell face first into that damn bush. It took four stitches to close the wound that almost got my eye, and my mother had Dad pull out the bush the next day.

□ ○ □

Grandma's wrinkled face left spaces in me that day. I tried to fill them with words, or movement of a hand as she did when she spoke—I couldn't do it. She cleared her throat and looked up from the depths of her glass. "You boys, Paul and you," she said and leaned on the table, moving her forearms over the surface, the empty water glass between them. "Your *matka* only has the two of you—even as naughty as you both are—but I have eight: seven boys and one girl—your *matka*. My husband die when your *matka* is thirteen—leaving me to do everything. Junie, my oldest boy, fall out of a car door, and is run over—drinking. Drunk. He come back from the big war II, and die, here." She flicked her arm back, abruptly. My Grandma's stories were always this way. I had to be patient until she found her way back on her own. She would wander, collecting bits and pieces from her past, allowing them to settle into her own time.

My mother told stories like Grandma did—hand movements and wanderings. When either my brother or I didn't want to go to school, she would click her tongue and we knew her school story was coming. "After Junie died, two years after my dad, I had to drop out of school. I was fifteen. I had to stay home and take care of my younger brothers, Joe and Carl, while Grandma worked." Then my mother would either go into how life was tougher or what it was like to live on Marquette Street—or anything else that didn't seem to have to do with not going to school. But she always finished with, "So, you two stay home and clean. I'll go to school."

"Your Uncle Stanley and Wally are no good. They don't help. Boys!" Grandma laughed, picking off a piece of lint that materialized on her blue housecoat. "I keep your *matka* home to take care of the little ones—I know she misses her friends at school, but what can I be doing? I have three jobs." She showed me her strong hands and counted three fingers for me. It was important I understand. "I am tough on your *matka*—you kids don't see." I got up and put my empty mug and dishes in the sink, rinsing them. Her voice followed me. "I love school, too. After the big war I, we have to build new schools and all us kids in one big room for a while. All doing different things: *matemática*, *gramática*, *historia*. I am sixteen and I love this boy, Alex." I turned around at that—this was the first time my grandma had spoken of such things. Always before it was just family: how she heard all but three of her brothers died during World War II; or what it was like on their farm, before she came to America.

I sat back down while my grandma paused. "Alex?" I asked.

"Yes, he had brown hair like you, but curly like your *matka*'s. He lived in the next village and I see him my first year, just before the new school is finish building, in . . . it's like high school, here."

I looked at the clock, it was almost noon . . . I had to be going soon. My mother would need the car. But I wanted to hear the rest, and I was wondering how to get the story back on track. I put in to help, "Paul told me he saw the school in Mauva—is it the new school he saw?" It was last year, on Paul's eighteenth birthday, she had taken him instead of me to Poland. Her own mother had died, at a hundred and three, forcing Grandma to go back. So Grandma, Paul, and Mother left me behind.

She sighed, "Yes. It is a three-mile walk for us kids from our village. Just before it is finish we are all in one room. I know of him from my friends from the other village—girls talking? Anyway, I love him, and he loves me too. We see each other all day at school and we meet on the weekends on the dirt road between our villages. We walk, holding hands—not like you kids here. Ah!" She scolded me, pointing a finger at me. She had seen me kissing a girl at one of my cousin's weddings. I blushed, not because I had been kissing a girl, but because, maybe, Grandma wanted to do those things and hadn't.

"He is thinking of going to Warsaw to finishing school, we call it there, to be an engineer. Alex is very smart and already the school is preparing him to go on. My *matka* hears that we love each other, everyone knows this, and is happy for me. My papa worry that Alex won't be able to take care of me for a long time, and Papa will have to." I heard the bitterness in her voice and realized she had never talked directly about her own father before. It was always her brothers or mother, or the farm. She saw my surprise.

"Ha, over there, then, girl marry by eighteen—take to live with the husband's family. My papa wonder how he can wait until Alex finish school. I can work hard, even harder than my lazy brothers—but I am the only girl in the family. My *matka* is always telling my papa things will be all right. But he doesn't think so . . . so, I don't marry Alex. I marry your grandpa, instead."

I could see this wasn't where she wanted to bring her story, but it seemed she had no choice. My mother had told me how Grandma came over on a boat, crowded to overflowing, with her husband. He was twenty years older than Grandma and she holding her three-year-old son, my dead Uncle Junie. That was when Grandma was nineteen, in 1921. But my mother's story seemed to be different—there was no bitterness, just the hope to make a better life in the new world: Grandpa dies when my mother is thirteen and she has to grow up to replace him.

"What about that man by the cow fence? When you were sixteen?" I asked.

"Ah, that man is my papa's second cousin." She didn't go on, instead she watched her hands—waiting.

"Oh," was all I could say.

"Before I come to America, on that boat with your grandpa and Junie, Alex give me a slip from a rose bush of his *matka's*." She got up and went to the sink and started washing the dishes. "It is getting late, I am not even dressing for the day yet . . . " she said, raising her voice above the running faucet.

"Did you end up meeting that man?" I asked to her back. She stopped for a second letting the running water fill in the silence before she answered.

"That man is your grandpa—my husband. But I don't know it until later when he come to dinner," she said, her voice rushing, blending with the water. "He is second cousin to Papa and that is how things are done there. My papa want to make things better . . . for everyone—that is how things are done: boys work the fields and your grandpa will take care of me." She sighed over the running water as if there was nothing more that needed to be said. "Now go do what you boys do. I have things to do and the morning is gone."

She turned off the water and wiped her hands dry on the corner of her housecoat. She went to the refrigerator and reached for her purse on top, clutching her robe to herself.

"No," I said, not quite understanding the questions that her story had left in me. "I enjoy coming here and helping."

"Oh, you are such a rich man?" She dug out a five dollar bill and put it in my hand, holding up the other hand to forestall any objection. "You work, you get pay. Now you won't be asking your *matka* for money." She picked up my coat from the chair and handed it to me. "Go, go. I do nothing today but talk—go."

I grabbed my coat and slipped it on. "Okay, Grandma, but next time it snows I'll come back and do your sidewalk for nothing."

"Yeah, yeah, you do that. *Dobre.* Tell your brother to stop to see me when he has more time, no?"

"Yes," I said and left.

□ ○ □

My mother never spoke of the rose bush and why she had it pulled out. My dad must've understood because he never said a word about it, either. One morning he just awoke early and went outside and cut it down. My brother and I came outside as he was digging up the roots.

We watched as he stabbed the ground with the shovel, twisting the point and snapping through roots and dirt, over and over again, until we became bored and wandered away to do other things, coming back occasionally to watch. My father worked at it most of the morning, took a break for lunch, then went back to finish in the afternoon. I didn't know, or couldn't understand, how deep those roots went. Finally, my father finished and filled in the hole with the old dirt and some fill. He stood there a minute, as Paul and I watched, silent, and wiped the sweat from his forehead with the back of a gloved hand. "I'd like to see him do that to the apple tree," I whispered to Paul.

"Shut up, Rafel," he said and punched me in the arm, hard.

My grandma never mentioned the bush or why it was gone. When she was over, or when we were at her house, there was an uneasiness that was hard for me to pinpoint. The tension of curt words that only Mother and Grandma understood, appearing to us as nothing more than thickness in their laughter—something that is only clear when it is looked back on. Something maybe Paul understood but I didn't, or maybe not, until they had come back from that trip to Poland. Then I should've understood.

It was hard to ignore my mother and Paul because they lived in the same house as me, but I didn't really speak to Grandma for almost that whole year. Paul was constantly talking of Poland, the places he had seen from Grandma's stories, and Mother joined in only when Paul needed added detail. But, for the most part, Mother seemed to understand my need for silence and rarely spoke of what the trip meant to her, and I never asked—I had wanted to see the places of Grandma's stories, and be a part of that more than anything—not Paul, or my mother.

Grandma asked me questions that needed more than a shrug of my shoulders or a "mmm" from me. I always tried to be looking at something else when she was speaking to me so I didn't have to look at her. And when I did see her face, she was always grinning. Maybe it wasn't for a whole year, I don't remember, but it seemed that way. Then, that winter when I was seventeen, I ended up shoveling her sidewalk all by myself. Paul never did take the time to visit—caught up in his own life. And in the spring, Grandma put a thin frail fence around the bottom half of her rose bush. To keep the rabbits from nibbling the base away, she told me. "When you marry and have a house," she said, waving her arm around, encircling her yard and garden. "I will give you a slip for your own yard."

III.
Things Never to Talk About

The Secret

I say a drunk missed my daughter, not killing her hours before. He missed her and hit a tree, I say—my neighbor's. He didn't hit my precious four year old who moments before was running in her new Barbie shoes—the pink ones with gold sparkles, the ones that left her feet and flew as if on a string. My wife didn't sink to her knees on the front lawn, slowly, frame by frame. She didn't pound her fists, or pull her hair. She is not sitting across from me with blood on her shirt.

No.

A circle was/is created and I am there/here holding the threads and . . . I say that the drunk misses my baby by . . . oh, four feet, hitting the neighbor's tree. He kills himself instead. The moment before he dies, the last tingle of life, he realizes what he almost did, a flashbulb before his eyes. He sees his life leaking away, and regrets *his* existence, which is about to end—not my daughter's. He looks up and sees me, watching him. The last thing he sees, before his eyes close forever, is me smiling.

Sarah, crying, runs to my arms. I press my relief into her downy hair. I wipe her eyes dry, then hug her to me. My fingers whiten. "It's OK hon, it's OK," I soothe her, and carry her back to the house. "Everything's OK, now."

"Helen!" I call to my wife who comes running from the house, her face white. "Look, she's OK. He missed her. She's here," I yell triumphantly. I hold her up, "In my arms, shaken, but safe."

The crowd of neighbors swarms over the wreck. I think I hear someone retch. Sirens shriek off in the distance. The ending of the day is bright.

My wife's face is undergoing the most amazing change—a look flitting away even as I watch her run up to us. The one that is now returning to whatever room it came from—the look you get when you realize that Mr. Reality is knocking at your door, and he brought along his old hooded friend for some dinner, and maybe a little wine, perhaps.

"Oh honey, oh honey," my wife chants as she encircles us both in her arms.

The police have just arrived. In the distance, more sirens are adding to the waning day's excitement: an ambulance maybe, or a fire truck (a little late, boys). I watch as they run up to the passenger door of the wreck, since the driver's side was now part oak tree. One cop, the fastest, gags from the smell of blood mingled with urine and feces, or what I call Eau de Death # 5.

"You okay, Jim?" I hear one of the slower cops say.

"Glaaaaah . . ." Jim responds.

"Guess not," another answers.

The ambulance has now added to the traffic of red lights, being followed closely by a fire truck. One of the smarter cops approaches us.

"Excuse me sir, but can I ask you a few questions?" he asks politely, glancing nervously over his shoulder at the car wrapped around the tree. Afraid, I guess, he'll be called over to help.

"Sure," I smile. "Why not? My name is Wilmer. Helen," I turn to my wife, "Take Sarah into the house, OK?" She leaves, still chanting.

I turn back to the cop, my smile threatening to leap off my face and slap him alongside the head. "What do you want to know?"

"Why are you smiling, bub?" he says, trying to act indignant.

I feel like toying with him, but I don't because I'm on the inside of this thing, and he isn't. It wouldn't be fair, and besides, I like his face: big, broad, openly innocent. He telegraphs every emotion he has right across his puss like a lighted billboard. He must lose his ass every time he plays poker.

"Well, Officer, it's like this: my daughter is playing on the sidewalk there," I point, "And I'm on the porch reading my newspaper . . . you following me?" My hands dance in front of his face like a magician weaving incantations.

He nods.

"And that asshole over there," I point to the car wrapped around the tree. His face starts to pinch with anger. "I'm sorry, Officer. I meant ex-asshole." My smile becomes granite. "Anyway, he comes swerving around the corner— there, jumping the curb—there," I point towards Bob's two-story brick. "He mows down Bob's petunias, misses the porch and . . . " I stop and squint, "God! I guess old rover won't be shitting on my lawn anymore. Bummer for Bob, though. Well, he then decides that Bob's yard wasn't enough so he tries out mine for size. But instead of going for any of the landscape, he decides to economize my family, giving us one less mouth to feed by heading for my Sarah." I choke a bit. My smile threatens to become something more mundane.

I hold on.

I can see that he is becoming a part of my secret now. I lean close, sharing another part. "Do you know, Officer," I look around making sure no one else is listening. I've hooked him—hooked him so deep it's probably sticking out his ass.

"Do you know that when you see your beloved child is about to be taken out—squashed like some insignificant insect by some uncaring, irresponsible human—that your heart almost stops. That your breath . . . um, by the way, if you don't mind my asking?" I ask, "What's your name?"

"William," he blurts, taken by surprise. "Bill to my friends."

"Bill," I say grasping his arm with my right hand, gesturing with my left. "Your breath stops here." I point to my throat. "You want to scream to high heaven, but you can't." My hand tightens on his arm (his big blue eyes grow). "You can feel your heart's next thump, waiting right behind that scream."

Bill and I are alone now, invisible to the others. We are one, bound by my secret—bound in a quilted fear of death. His young face is now reliving the terror with me. We are linked by my hand on his arm.

"Billy boy, my daughter's short life flashed before my eyes." My voice becomes my passion, and my words become windows. "Bill, in that wayside out of time, I saw her born. I watched her take her first steps," rushing now, unable to contain the words, "I heard her say 'Da Da,' saw the first glass of milk spilled, diapers, first pictures, felt tiny hands caressing my ear—Don't you see? Don't you see?" I'm welded to his arm.

"Yes," he moans.

"I could see her running to me with an owie to kiss. Are you one with me, Billy boy? Do you understand?"

"Yes, oh yes," he whispers, open face, with eyes beginning to focus with a pinpoint fire.

"I saw what could've been wasted. Wasted!" I am exalted. I release his arm. "Anyway, Bill," I sigh, "the car missed my daughter by four feet, then hit Sylvia's oak tree," I point next door.

Composing himself a little, he says, "Yes, I see . . . missed your daughter by four feet, then hit the tree. Probably drunk."

"Yes, no doubt. Now dead—instead of my daughter."

"Yes!" he whispers fiercely. He is now a disciple of the secret. My first. "Mr. Wilmer?"

"Tom to my friends." I nod.

"Tom, does your family need any help? A doctor for your daughter?"

"No, Bill, my wife and I can handle it from here. But thanks anyway."

"Are you okay, Ryan?" I hear in the background.

"Glaaaah . . . " Ryan replies.

"You could do me a favor, though?"

"Just ask, Tom."

"When this is all over . . . you could call on us. Dinner maybe? Some conversation, huh?"

"I'd like that Tom. I'd like that just fine."

"Great." We shake hands. "I won't keep you from your job, Officer."

"Good day, Mr. Wilmer." He walks away.

I watch as he marches up to the wreck. I see the look of disdain he holds for his gutless comrades. His lips suppress a smile. My smile. The radios crackle with nonsense while the red lights, twirling, blinking, add an accent of invulnerability to him. He glides forward through the spinning chaos, looks into the car, tightens his lips lest the smile jump off *his* face. Hands on hips, he turns to the others who are awed by his courage and control.

"Get this piece of shit out of here!"

Sarah gets over her shock, with our love being heaped upon her, surrounding her in a cloak of gentleness, and she grows into womanhood sure of herself, respectful of us, and we can't love her enough, or too much, and she goes to Harvard, gets her law degree, and graduates at the top of her class, and she becomes the youngest woman to be appointed to the Supreme Court, and then she is talked into running for president of the US and she wins and she brings the world peace and she dies at one-hundred-twenty years old, ten years after we pass on.

The circle is complete. It begins again and I direct thread around me. The wind ruffles my newspaper. The tires hitting the curb sound like old glass breaking, over and over again. The screaming begins—behind me, in front of me—I wonder out loud how I'll ever finish reading the newspaper.

Partial Recovery

The boy's hand felt like liquid fire in mine. So many things change when you get older, like heart attacks and your hands, and it was as if his life was burning out of them—I imagined him as a lightbulb. I gently took my hand away, selfish of my old wrinkled-self, and shuffled back to my bed. I had to be careful not to tangle the tubes running from my chest: tubes feeding antibiotics and anticlotting agents.

I sat down on the bed and clasped my hands together. They felt like crinkled waxed paper, and my weak pulse stuttered within them. I was sure the boy had a strong heart. I had felt it beating through his palms—strong and sure. Unlike his heart, mine was on the fritz.

I wondered if I would trade places with the boy for his strong heart and burning hands. I knew he was dying of something—cancer, maybe, or some other whispered disease. I wasn't sure. But maybe that "not knowing" what's killing you would be better than a lousy ticker. As I stared at the boy's closed eyes, I wondered if he would trade for a bad heart and cold, scratchy hands. Maybe a bad heart was as strange to him as his disease was to me. I had an urge to pull out every tube and wake up the boy to show him, "See, this isn't so bad. They come out, no problem."

My wife, Bonnie, would be back up later, she had said. To console me. Those weren't the words, but they may as well have been. She was a professional—at funerals, and when my son moved as far as he possibly could—she con- soled. I loved her, but it was a tenuous thing and now I need- ed something, not that.

The boy moaned in his sleep—a sleep created by fever and drugs. I stared at him in his sleep, as I used to stare at my own son when he slept. His parents, he had told me before he drifted off, couldn't make it because of the snow storm that stifled the city. "From up north," he said as if being up north was as far as people could get from their sick little boys. I reluctantly went over to him as he struggled with his pain and loneliness, and held his hand until he slept. I didn't even know his name.

Yesterday, when I first woke up in my room from my open-heart surgery, I found that my eyes and mouth shared a dryness. The first thing I focused on was the small, skinny boy next to me. He stared intently at me, wondering, I thought, if I would make it out of my fugue.

He pointed a pale arm at the table beside my bed. "Water," he said and smiled. I reached over, until my fingers touched the cool cup that had been set there for just this purpose. "I'm always so thirsty after my surgeries," he said with such certainty, and experience, that I finally focused on him. He was bald. The fuzz above his eyes told me that he would be blond if he had hair. He had the most penetrating blue eyes, and that bothered me.

I wanted to tell him to mind his own business—who was he to look at me like that? Another thing disturbed me, I was supposed to have a private room. What was this young boy doing here with me? He stared at me openly and curi- ously, but he didn't say any more. He nodded wisely and turned his back to me. I listened to his breath going in and out, incredibly loud to me. The nurse came in and gave me a shot for pain. I went to sleep listening to the raspy rhythm of his breathing.

The nurses came and went, all that day, with efficiency. Pulse, blood pressure, and temperature—the same with the boy. I watched them when they attended him. I was hoping to catch a glimpse of what ailed him. I figured that the nurses' attention to his body would reveal his illness. The loss of hair was a tip-off, but still, I wasn't sure. I slept most of the time.

I watched him sleep as he must've watched me sleep, that first day. I watched his chest rise in the unrhythmic echo of his breathing. The skin of his face and his neck was a pink fire. His eyelids were red. Bonnie came in as I wondered at the boy. "He's sleeping," she stated the obvious.

"Yes," I said. "Had a tough time of it . . . I guess." I shrugged away the questions I knew she wanted to ask. "The nurse said that I'd be moved tomorrow . . . some sort of mix-up. . . . "

"Remember Bobby at that age. . . ?" she whispered. I was going to tell her not to bother whispering—they had shot the boy up with enough medication to put a rhino to sleep, the nurse said anyway. I kept quiet and watched Bonnie's face: scrunch, pinch, voila!—pity.

"I don't know how old he is—maybe ten." I moved higher in my bed. My chest was starting to hurt. I didn't want any painkillers yet—I didn't want to give in to Bonnie's pity.

"Is Robert coming?" I said. My ribs twinged with renewed pain.

"Tomorrow . . . the airports are all closed because of the snow."

"Ugh." My pain forced me to respond.

"Well, I see you're hurting, and the roads are getting real bad. I'll be going." She rose to her feet, stopped to say more, and didn't.

"Bye," I said. "And thanks."

She smiled weakly and left. The boy slept on. My own boy was somewhere, coming tomorrow. The boy's parents were somewhere and coming tomorrow.

I'd called Robert the day before my surgery, to remind him. "I'm going in tomorrow. The doctor said bypasses are different today. Shouldn't be a problem." I left it hanging, hoping he wouldn't hear the urgency in my voice—to see him. Just in case.

"I'll try to be there, Dad," he said. "I'll really try."

The doctor had said, "routine." "We're lucky we caught the blockage before you had a heart attack," he said, tapping his pencil on my chest X-ray. "Your heart has paid the price of too much abuse. You were lucky." I was/am lucky. I knew it. Most of my colleagues were suffering from all the pleasures they had indulged in, thinking as I did that *we* were forever.

"Call Bobby," Bonnie had said after the day was set for the surgery.

"Why bother him?" I said. "It's routine." But in the end I had called him. Afraid to call him. Afraid to tell him so he'd come see me. Afraid he wouldn't—couldn't make it. And the boy next to me, alone as I was, probably dying and not understanding the distances, and snow storms that kept people away.

The nurse came in and checked on the boy, and I almost asked then what the little boy had that made his hands so hot—but I couldn't. I was afraid of disturbing his sleep. She came over to me. "Would you care for anything?" she whispered.

"Something for the pain," I said, trying to pull myself higher in the bed. She reached a soft, cold hand out and helped me to get more comfortable. I could smell the lotion on her hand. "And some fresh water." I nodded toward my empty pitcher.

"Sure," she said, and plucked up my pitcher on the way out. A few moments later she appeared and silently pushed a needle in my arm, and set a full glass of water next to me. "Tomorrow, maybe late afternoon, we'll move you to a new room." She smiled and left. I was filling up with clouds and starting to drift off to sleep. I realized that I hadn't even bothered to ask her about the boy's condition. I realized in my selfish sleep that I didn't care.

I awoke, and again I had the feeling of dryness. The boy was propped high in his bed. The lights were low in the room and the TV blinked in silence. He, again, was searching me with his eyes. I smiled and grabbed the glass of water to show him I was as seasoned as he was. He nodded.

"Do you mind if I turn up the sound?" He pointed to the TV with his blue eyes. "I like this show."

"No. I mean, go ahead." I raised the head of my bed until I felt a twinge of a reminder from my chest. "What are you watching?"

"It's about wolves," he said, still with his serious boy face. I realized I had only seen him smile once—when I came out of my fugue. When I came back to the world. I shrugged to myself—not my concern.

"Tomorrow, I'll be leaving," I said, suddenly, then felt my face flush with the guilt for saying that.

"I know. The nurse told me." He smiled shyly and lowered his head to his chest.

I wanted to ask him if he knew the nurses' names, and how long he'd been here and why he would say nurse and not Mary, or Sylvia, and why the hell didn't he know their names? I wanted to tell him Bobby once broke his leg when he was ten, and spent the night at St. Luke's. He knew all the nurses by name when we came to pick him up. I was determined not to let it bother me.

"Do you like wolves?" he asked.

"What?" I'd heard him, but the question had nothing to do with names. What was his name? "Yes, I like wolves,"

I said and not, "My name's Robert—just like my son's, and what's your name?"

"Me, too," he said. "Did you take your son to the zoo . . . when he was little?"

My son? What did he know of *my* son? The barrier that I had built up, unknowingly, between us was being probed. I shored it up.

"My dad brought me to the zoo a lot," he said. He said in his old little voice. My resolve wavered.

"Yes." Then, "You like the zoo," I said. He nodded as if to say, "You're the one leaving tomorrow. Your turn." I nodded. "We lived a few miles from the zoo—I took Bobby there a lot, also." There, names. I waited for his, now. I didn't want it. There was a responsibility in names.

"We live 'bout a hour and a half away. Even before," he hesitated looking for the proper words, "Even before *here*, we'd drive to the zoo—hour and a half."

"Bobby's favorite were the monkeys. We'd sit for hours watching the monkeys." I nodded toward the TV: a pack of wolves were loping in the snow. "The roads should be clear by tomorrow," I said.

He nodded. "My favorite were the polar bears. Big and all white," he said. "When I was young, my dad took me to the zoo and every animal we saw I'd ask, 'do they bite?'"

He said "young" not "younger." Was he that old? I wondered.

"My dad said that he got so sick of telling me if they did or not, that he just said 'no' to everything." The boy smiled again. My ribs were starting to hurt. "Then, when I was older, when I came down here for treatments, we'd go to the zoo. My dad and I made it a joke. 'Dad,' I'd say, 'Do the lions bite?' and he'd say, 'No, lions don't bite' and we'd laugh."

I wondered what his father answered when the boy asked him if he would die? The boy was still talking. I let him.

"Every time we came here, we went to the zoo. Even in the winter. The polar bears seemed thicker in the winter, and more," he searched again for the right word, and the wolves running in the snow turned into the mountains of someplace I didn't catch, "more active."

I closed my eyes as he told me of the zoo. I could hear the boy's voice, younger somehow, asking questions of his dad. Bobby asked me when he had broken his leg, "Will I run again?"

I had laughed, relieved. "Of course."

"We go to the polar bears last, because it's somehow the best." His fuzzy eyebrows scrunched up, probably trying to place the mountains on TV, too. "'Do they bite? Do they bite. . . ?' my dad always says, in my voice, when we get there. I say, in his, 'Nooo, polar bears don't bite.'"

He almost said his name. I was waiting for it. I sighed.

Bobby always would ask me, too, if something or another would bite you—"If you got too close, would it bite?" Would it? I remember my impatience, and wished that we could've laughed, too. Made a joke between a father and son. But Bobby wasn't here, dying, and I wondered what the boy's father said—had said. "Do polar bears bite, Dad? and will I die? Do they Dad?"

No. Maybe. I don't know. Ask your mother, for chrissakes!

"I'm tired," I said. I'll be gone tomorrow, I thought, and my chest hurt, and then the room became silent.

I rang the nurse for something for pain.

HeShe

The home pregnancy test sat opened on the kitchen table. He lay his coat over a chair and tried to see if it was empty. He couldn't tell. How's your day? She asked. Fine, fine, He said—not, did you do it already? Are you? Aren't you?

How was yours? He said, purposely not looking at the box on the table. OK, I guess. She was cutting carrots over the sink. She pushed away the hair that kept tickling the side of her face. The filtered rays of the sun lay coldly over the box—as if it were a sundial.

Shopping today? He said. Yes, we needed some things, She said. She diced up the remaining carrots and dumped them unceremoniously into the roasting pan. She added a sprinkle of salt over the small roast that lay there. She hesitated before putting the cover on, and added a pinch more. He watched her do this as He watched the box at the same time.

Did you get some more soap? He said. She blew at the hair that wouldn't stop its attack on her face. Of course. She pushed the pan with the roast lying in it into the oven. He wanted to ask her if She used it? If the box was empty—as simple as that. *Is the box empty?* would tell him the half of it. What else did you buy? He tried to sound uninterested. Things, She said, blowing at the hair.

How long till dinner, He said. An hour or so . . . that is if you want it tender? Of . . . course, He said, then, tomorrow is my turn—how about chicken? Chicken's fine, She smiled. He then grabbed her in his arms. At first She lay limp against him, but the urgency of his grip made her grab back—just as hard.

He watched the box on the table and the sun silently caressing it.

He kissed her neck, warm from cutting up vegetables. An hour? He murmured into her warm neck. An hour, She said. She pulled him away from the kitchen toward the bedroom. They moved with each other's feet between the other's—dancing to the bedroom. He tried one last time to see if the box was empty. She pulled him into the room—onto the bed—pulling his shirt out of his pants. The room was getting dark as the sun fell toward tomorrow. They pulled each other's clothes off, frantically as if to beat the darkness and the roast.

Naked, He on top, She on the bottom, they clasped and sweated. She bit his shoulder—He entered her. Water, the taste of the ocean ran from them, down the bed, to the floor. The sun's rays became streams, mixing with the salt of their bodies—running down in streaks. The room filled with water—over the lip of the bed. Over them, as they frantically loved—filling the whole room with dark, salt water. They became still. Holding onto each other, cold, lying there. In the kitchen, the cold sunlight filtered over the box, not through, and just lay there.

Hunter's Moon

Joy Marie thought she could hear the child crying—in the distance. Crying for her mother. I hope to God, she told herself, the child can still cry. But then she put that thought out of her head; the child was alive and only just lost.

Jim had taken Moon and was searching the far side of the ravine, along with the father and other men and their dogs. She was left with the mother, other women, some who had small children of their own, and a couple teenagers to search the field. The child had been gone for eight hours, since two in the afternoon, the tear-streaked mother kept reminding them as each hour passed. She will be cold. She only had on a light fall jacket, you know, the kind you can buy at K-mart for $9.99—blue-light special. "She is eight and will be so cold," the mother repeated as if the telling would hurry the search.

As if it needed to be, thought Joy Marie. She wanted to tell the mother to quiet down, relax. They were almost as frantic as she was to find the child. Some of the women looked over their shoulders at the mother, and Joy Marie could see all their children, or prospective ones—in the eyes, as wide as moons, thanking God at the same time that it wasn't their children they were searching a bright moonlit field for. The field was golden in the moonlight and the searchers were faintly luminescent, whispering to each other, as if afraid to be recognized.

Joy Marie didn't have a daughter, or son, and was now thinking that maybe Jim was right and they shouldn't bring kids into this world. Though he had been fantasizing lately, ever since they had moved from Milwaukee, that maybe life in the country would be quiet and good for kids. She didn't want to search nightmares on full moons—Hunter's Moon, it was called—for her children. Jim was with the county sheriff and it was five years since he was a cop in Milwaukee. She was finally sleeping nights, not waiting for the phone to ring. Crime and shit don't come to places like theirs, she thought angrily.

The women were moving toward the lip of the ravine and spreading the word in whispers that matched the trampled grass to spread out parallel to the edge and work their way to the quarry. Dogs were barking across the shadow of the ravine, and she could hear the deep "woof" of Moon and Jim's voice calling after him. Some of the women paired off, holding hands and disappearing into the tall grass. Support, thought Joy Marie, God what if we find. . . ?

The girl, child, had been last seen playing behind the mother and father's house. Right off of Ken Bauer's land. She must've wandered into the fields, after a ball maybe? Or, maybe down into the ravine that ended in a cul-de-sac at the rock quarry where she was told again and again never to go. All the mothers, and yet-to-be ones, had shaken their heads and clucked their tongues—yes, find her first, then comfort. Then punish so she doesn't ever ever do this again. This wasn't spoken, but Joy Marie had heard it. It was in their movements, their eyes, and she could hear it in their heart-beats as they moved across the field. She hoped the child's heart still beat—fast and afraid, waiting to be found.

Not a one mentioned foul play, but Joy Marie saw it stamped all over Jim's face when he told her that a child was missing, presumed lost; lost to the "new" family that just moved onto a parcel of Bauer land. And, they needed volunteers to search Bauer's fields. "New" was a relative term in Dodge County. She knew immediately to whom Jim was referring. Although the family had been there two years, they were the new family until someone else moved into the community. Neither Joy Marie nor Jim would put a name to the family. Foul play, Jim's face said. In our no-place county we have foul play, more than you would know, Joy Marie, and I can't give a foul-played family a name. Of course Jim never said that, but she had heard it nonetheless—in his not naming the child, though she heard it enough tonight echoing off the walls of the ravine. Heard it as she heard his blood flow.

The child's name was being called continuously across the field, almost in a chant, a hope of conjuring the girl. During the day the parents had searched the first couple hours themselves: he on County Trunk "G" in his car, and she by Bauer's apple orchard, east of the ravine and the quarry, which lined the long gravel drive going back to Bauer's home. The mother wasn't frantic yet, it was still warm for October, and there was light. They were embarrassed to alarm anyone. But when night was coming on, colder and deeper, they had called Jim and told him the child was missing. Joy Marie listened to the child's name being called, but couldn't bring herself to say that name aloud.

The field was lit with the moon-sunlight—almost like day. The field bent before her with a snarl of dried-up grass, and she could hear Jim's voice echoing in the ravine, calling for Moon. Up ahead she heard the frantic calling of someone, a mother, or prospective one, for sure. Jim's call for the dog echoed in her head. She thought about the word "moon." You could draw it out forever and never say the "n," and people would still know the word was "moon."

Moon: a large ball of bright nothing in the sky, a lanky dog who rarely minded her or Jim, a word that echoes and cries in the night.

The rush of bodies, pushing through the grass to catch up to the frantic calls, passed by and left her behind. Calls of "Here," and "No, stay back," were heard—in the air to grasp if Joy Marie wanted. Jim's voice still echoed out of the night.

Someone had definitely found something. Everyone was rushing to the place, but Joy Marie suddenly felt tired and alone. She sat down heavily and leaned back on her elbows. She noticed that the tips of her shoes were covered with a dust from the dry grass. A dog named Moon was enough—she definitely didn't want to have children. They cry and are always underfoot, or lost, or may become involved in foul play.

Jim's voice was getting closer and she stared at the huge moon. There were shouts and more shouts from ahead. She waited to find out what foul play had been played. The sound of Jim's voice pushed into the sky, echoing in her mind—*moon*—almost like a child's crying.

Sisters

Gina receives the letter on her seventeenth birthday from the dead woman, again, postmarked from England. She puts it in the shoe box she keeps under her bed. The letters started coming six years ago—she has six, now, folded neatly. In her mind far from Canada, she begins humming a song that belongs to the past and South Africa—Sis, a black girl from the village, taught it to her—clapping her pale hands in time to forgotten music. Her memories of Sis are of warm hands—black hands. And those memories usually come back when she receives the letter. Her brother, Royce, reads his letters and even writes back. This she knows hurts her father who has never forgiven the woman for abandoning them—but he never says.

Gina refuses to spend time reading them, or waste paper writing back to someone who is dead.

"She wants you to write," Royce said to her in her room. "She is terribly hurt." Gina knew these must be the dead woman's words because Royce never says "terribly." The woman must be dead to say things that neither she nor Royce ever said. She stared past him, pulling her brush through her long hair, and started humming her and Sis's song. "Why won't you write her?" Royce said, blowing out his breath, grabbing her arm. "She's sorry. She's our mother. She wants to see us." He squeezed her arm in his urgency, shaking her gently as a warm dry breeze might. She stared at him with smoky eyes.

"She is dead, Royce. We don't have a mother." She swayed with the humming in her head and the pull of Royce's hand.

"Damn you, Gina!" He fled from her, slamming the door behind him.

Sis and she were playing by the water tank her father had just built for the village. Since people had to go all the way to the river, her father had built it to "make life easier"—another string of words that were alien to her. Sis opened the valve that was just above their heads, and began dancing under it, letting the water splash over her dusty, black body—making her shine like a beautiful fish. Gina became indignant as only a five year old could, and demanded Sis turn it off. Didn't her father work hard to give the village water?

Sis, being older, smiled and laughed at her, the water rolling over her thick lips. "Foolish," she said in the language the two of them found together. She squirmed her toes deep in the mud forming at her feet. "My father say, 'let white man play—river gives us water. Not man or tank.'" She stamped her feet and clapped. "We not lazy."

Since Gina was only five, she forgot the reasons why the tank was so important. Sis opened the valve wider and held out her hand to Gina. "Come 'Na. I'll teach you a song." Her long fingers beckoned Gina under the falling water. Gina reached out and, hand in hand, they danced under the cool water. Sis started singing, "Water in the river, plenty river run—white man's tank only for fun—run water, run water, never go—'Na dance, till water's slow."

Her father was always working. A man who needed to move his hands and build things. He never talked to her of the past, of his work in South Africa, or of their reason for coming to Canada—and Gina never asked. It seemed that when he spoke of things farther than ten years ago, his lips fumbled through the words. It was as if his lips couldn't remember the past.

Royce was the one who always wanted to remember the past (though she never listened). He was the one who tried to tie strings to places and people that were gone. He constantly told, to those who would listen, of the night they fled in the bush with their houseboy, hurrying to gather the things to take. And told of how he sneaked his race car set that he was *forbidden* to take (but did anyway). Royce told of the frantic look of their mother (Gina wouldn't hear) at leaving everything behind, and of being led into the bush by the houseboy (they called them servants in Canada). Hiding in the bush, sleeping on the car seats—the strange looks from the villagers for them being white.

Royce was the one that wanted to remember the "woman" because Gina couldn't—wouldn't, because, like black-and-white photos taken long ago, her memories faded with the years into still lifes: their father mounting the water tank, his face red from the sun with the look that he wished he could do more: the woman standing before him, poised as if to run.

The revolution was still going on over there, she learned in school. "Wasn't she there?" someone asked her. She shook her head no. She only had the wrinkled up, pocket memories of South Africa that folded out sometimes to let her glimpse what had gone before. Still, for some reason, she thought of that place as home.

Gina felt at home in the village. At least until she was around her father and the woman who looked lost. When she was five, she couldn't have put the words to the faces around her. It wasn't until she was older, and the memories came unasked for, that she was able to make the connection.

Gina turned fourteen. She and her father went to see a Shakespeare play at the Montreal Arts Theater. She enjoyed going places with him. Without Royce along, her father seemed to breathe with less effort. He even smiled more, stretching the years and sun from his face. They sat in the front row, lightly holding hands. King Lear was on stage, his face was disfigured, and he was making a long speech. Then, as if the stage were a projector, her past began to dance in her eyes: Her father and the woman shouting over a lost gun (?)—who took it!? Royce? No, he'd have brought it back after he showed it off. Someone else? Why? Their eyes darting around the small dirty hut, taking inventory of their things, lest they too would disappear. Then the woman storming out, glaring at her father, and her father lying on the car seat that became a bed, covering up his face with his arms. The scene ended and applause erupted. She expected her father to stand and bow.

She received her first letter when she was eleven, when South Africa was only a tugging string and not yet a hungry memory. She came home from school and her father was at the table, holding a cup of coffee in his large, dry hands. He was staring at the maid's back as she did the dishes—a white woman from the US. He refused to hire blacks to do menial work.

"Gina, come sit with me," he said. His voice triggered, for the first time, the humming of Sis, "'Na 'Na." Sis couldn't say Gina's whole name. And Gina couldn't even come close to repeating Sis's African name, so she just called her Sis—Gina wanted a sister, anyway.

"A letter came for you." He wouldn't look at her. He smiled faintly as if the maid were doing something amusing. He pushed the letter to Gina without looking.

She took it in her hands, rubbing her fingers over the outside; feeling the letter inside. "A letter, Daddy?" she said. "From who? Africa?" She didn't know why she suddenly thought it from Africa—maybe it was the humming that was starting in her head; the childish idea that Sis had written her. It never occurred to her that it was probably impossible that Sis would know where she was. Her father's head snapped up, and for a moment, she thought she saw Africa in his eyes. She thought he would hit her, then Canada replaced it. His face became pulled and tired.

She thought she could see the heat shimmering on him as she remembered from long ago.

"Honey, it's postmarked from England. London." He *squeezed his eyes in the bright sun. "I think . . . I know . . . It's* from your mother." *Her father's hands went to his face to mop the sweat that was forming there. The* whump whump *of a helicopter could be heard in the distance—coming from the village. Gina's father hid her and Royce in the brush by the river where they had been fishing. The black children who tagged along to watch started running to see the helicopter. She wanted to go, but he pushed her into Royce's arms. "Stay!" he yelled above the thumping. He followed the black children back. They crouched in the brush, Royce crushing her to him. Whump whump. She squirmed free, running after her father, tears streaking her face. Drying as she ran. Whump whump, it was getting louder. She ran harder. She was sobbing. Then, the woman running for the helicopter that seemed to have appeared out of the dust and sun. Her father screaming for the woman to come back, "They might be rebels. Kill us all." The woman not hearing, or wanting to. Running slow motion, arms raised above the tall grass—running almost falling. Gina calling out to wait, the helicopter smothering her voice into sand. The woman too far to hear, or see, her. Running and disappearing in the brush and the* whump whump *becoming louder—then she heard Sis's warm dusty hands, clapping 'Na 'Na 'Na.*

"She's dead—dead," Gina said, simply. "She died in Africa." Taking the unopened letter with her, she went to her room, walking stiffly as if her legs were iron pegs. She emptied her new shoes out of their box and gently laid the letter inside. Then, softly putting the cover on, she slid the box underneath her bed.

Gina and her father never spoke of the woman, or of South Africa, or why Royce refused to stop reading letters from a dead woman. She received another, then another, and put them one on top of the other in the shoe box. Each year she slid the dust-covered box out to receive its mail, then put it back to lie until the next one. Not even caring the least bit what a dead person had to say.

They always came right on her birthday, not a day before or after. Like today, she thinks. Then, for some reason, she wonders if they came before she was eleven. Maybe her father didn't give them to her because he felt she was too young. Next year she will graduate from high school and go on to college. Maybe in the States. And she will burn all the letters and bury the ashes in the garden.

She sits in front of the mirror pulling a brush through her hair, not really looking at her reflection, which reminds her of someone else. She wonders if Sis had ever married. Maybe she was. They got married young there. Sis's hair was short and knotty—hers is long and straight. She hears that the revolution has touched all areas and tribes. She hopes Sis is still living.

The Red Cross helicopter lands close to the village, pushing up dust, blowing the tops off some of the huts. Her father rushes out of theirs, his face searching for the woman's—for her to rush out to meet him and his children. Instead, white people and other colored people—not black—leap from the doors, ducking the blades. "Have you seen my wife?" her father screams at each face that comes close enough to his. "Have you seen my wife?" Royce runs around, enjoying the dust that flies wildly in circles. Gina hides in the doorway, afraid of the helicopter—afraid to get sucked away like the woman did. Royce mounts the doorway with the help of a stranger's hand. She searches for Sis. Is Sis going, too?

Her father, face tight and pinched, pulls her away from the door-
way, screaming, and puts her into the helicopter.

Gina sits in front of the mirror, clapping her hands, and wonders if she can remember the whole song that she and Sis made up together. She claps her hands, picking up the beat, chanting the words as she remembers them. As the words come back to her, she wonders, if Sis were dead, would Sis write, too?

IV.
Last One for the Long Road

Since Then

Hard fought truth chiseling faces fear
pushing drunken metaphor
squeezing more black from night
time is too large a concept too gray
like truth a big ball of stone
that's more like it stone
begging for mercy
stone is truth stone time
how many has it been?
In front of me to the side overhead
always at my heels since then stone
mute merciless familiar.

Amy E. De Jarlais

Sunday Nights Down at the Rusty Nail

In Nowhere, Wisconsin, the Sunday night is just too damn hot to spend in your little, two-room apartment. So you go on down to the Rusty Nail for a cold one and hope tomorrow is better. In fact, you're hoping everything gets better, because you're unemployed. And between the rent on your cracker-box apartment, and the small amount of food you buy, your unemployment check just won't stretch from Monday to Monday, much less hot Sunday nights. But still you go to join the ranks of the hot.

The bar is full of lost souls like you who can't afford air-conditioning, or they use the heat as an excuse to drink. You plop your tired, hot ass between Bill and Harvey even though there are lots of open stools. On the other side of the small U-shaped bar, the old-timers sit staring at you. But you know they're not really looking, and if they are, you don't care. The smell of used beer spilt on the floor, bar, and on Bill and Harvey, makes you thirsty. The stale cigarette smoke that lingers in the air from nights past gives the bar a smell of permanence you can understand—not like a job. Not like a marriage.

Harvey and Bill seem delighted you've shown up. Bill asks where've you been. Nowhere, you tell him. Harvey's already drunk—Harvey was hot early today. The smile on his face is lopsided from the beer he's been drinking—and that also makes you thirsty. The light is soft as smoke, and the air-conditioning feels good on your face.

You grab Donny's attention. A beer here, you wave, pointing to the empty space in front of you like you're landing planes. The peanut shells scatter before your hands to make a smooth runway for Donny to land your beer. The TV is up on the wall behind the old men, competing with the country music vibrating off of the jukebox—some tune about a job gone bad. You can relate to that. You toast the jukebox.

Right after you'd lost your job, your wife decided it was time for her to find herself. You sip your beer and sincerely hope she found herself underneath a truck's tire on Highway 41. Or maybe she found that it was the house payments, and car payments, washer-dryer-doctor payments, that spilled over and washed her out the door to find a job, a life. Without you, of course.

The TV has some foreign sports game playing on it, something to do with kicking a ball around. But it's not soccer—you know soccer. There are never good sports on Sunday TV, now that the football season is over. The old men hunch underneath the TV, not bothering to turn around to see, and chew their memories over and over to each other, unaware that there is more to sports than football.

You were fired from Alma Corporation six months ago because they no longer needed human hands to do your job: progress, they'd told you. Now at thirty-five, you're just not ambitious enough to be let down again. Fifteen years of your life you've given them. You even voted against a union! Now you're wishing you would've voted "yes." But who knew that human hands were no longer good enough? And that thirty-five was old?

Surely not Joe, your old shift partner who had been there as long as you had. Once he told you that he would die before he joined a union. Fuckers'll take your money, he'd always say, then kill you if you don't listen to what they tell you. Last week you'd heard he was working for Mercury, a union shop. If you could just get off your ass, you'd be happy to work for Mercury, too.

Bill says something about shooting dice for a shot. You say, why the hell not. You turn to Harvey and ask, you in? In all the frickin' way, he burps out. You knew he was, it was like a ritual every Sunday night, dating back to the beginning of Sundays. He says that every time, and acts as if it's the first—it's only the same-old, same-old.

Bring 'em out, you tell Bill. He's been fondling the dice box for a while—waiting. Comin' out, he shouts as if he needs to be heard. You don't know what Bill's trip in life is, but you'd heard he was run over by a car when he was younger. The driver, you'd also heard, had been drunk—and so had Bill. You guess it was probably a question of right of way, and the driver won hands down. Bill can't father children, something to do with a lack of parts—the main ones—so he drinks. And, you'd heard his wife went to find herself, too.

He spills out four 6s and pushes the dice box to you. You spill out three 5s and nudge Harvey that it's his turn. Harvey doesn't spill shit, so Bill's out, and it's between you and Harvey to see who buys the shot. Donny has changed the TV station to the ten o'clock news.

A couple of the old-timers have gotten up to shoot pool. Somehow, there are now twelve old men sitting on the other side of the bar (that's including the two shooting pool). You haven't noticed any more coming in, so you figure they're multiplying like amoebas. Amoebas, you laugh to yourself. You like the comparison: twelve this hour, twenty four next hour, then . . .

Harvey slaps the dice in front of you, making you blink your eyes. Beat four 5s, bud, he bellows in triumph, horse on you. So now you have a horse on you . . . it's probably better than having Harvey on you.

Harvey looks like a walrus from the Saturday morning cartoons you used to watch as a kid, mustache and all. Except this walrus is wearing a ketchup-stained T-shirt that says "Bartenders Do It Better," at least you think it's ketchup. Harvey is a slob. He takes the Friday and Saturday night shifts for Donny, then drinks his brains and money out on Sundays. You glance back at the TV wondering how much this round will cost you if you lose.

The news is on, you see. The volume is turned too far down to make out what the newscaster is saying. But you don't need sound to hear what's up. You can fill in the words yourself: man killed in two car collision . . . five die in fire . . . today in a war somewhere that we started for no apparent reason, one hundred men, women, and innocent children died. The stupidity goes on. You don't know why they just don't nuke the world and have done with it.

The old men have finished their game of pool and are back lined up, like a jury, at the bar again. You can see yourself going over there and giving them all a Three Stooges slap. Right down the line. Now you laugh a little too loud and Harvey turns a big hairy eyeball on you. What's so fun . . . funny? he demands, pointing to his dice. Beat that, laughing boy!

You reach for the dice again and notice on TV that the roving reporter from Channel Six is in a church somewhere. Some suburb. Oh yeah! you remember. That's where the face of Jesus Christ is supposed to have appeared on the wall. You spill out the dice—you've lost. Harvey is doing his walrus laugh in your ear, teetering on his stool—you feel like shoving a fish in his mouth. Jesus in suburbia, how appropriate. You swallow the rest of your beer.

Bill declares blackberry brandy to be the drink of the game. You yell for Donny to set them up. Except for Bill's declaration he is silent; you didn't even remember he was sitting next to you. Donny appears—three shots and a beer, you say, shaking your head.

Jesus would never show His face around this place, you ponder—too boring. If He did, it would probably be above the jukebox on the wall, since it played the saddest music on Sundays—not like the stuff that rumbles out on Friday and Saturdays. Harvey pushes you to drink the shot Donny has set up. You notice your small pile of bills has just gotten smaller—thanks to Donny and the dice. The blackberry brandy goes down like wine.

Harvey pushes the dice box back in front of you. You bring 'em out, you lost—he can hardly talk, now. Bill is sullen, staring into his beer. You can't tell if he's drunk or not. On the TV, the people are pressing into the church. You see the eager looks on their faces—that look is one you understand—hope. Hope that the heat doesn't get shut off in the winter, and that the phone ringing isn't the bill collector.

Ten dollars a day, Bill whispers. What's that? you ask him. Ten dollars a day, he repeats, I clean the bar for ten dollars a day. You wonder if he's talking to you. Things could be worse, you tell him, at least you have a job. I want to die— you've heard him say this before. C'mon Bill, you put in helpfully. Look at me, I'm broke! He continues to mumble. You ignore him.

Now, on the TV, they're showing the wall where Jesus's face is supposed to be. You don't see anything there. The bar suddenly feels hot. The hypocrites! you want to shout, shaking the old men out of their chewing. Here, it dawns on you, are the real people, not like those in the church. Here, people know who and what they are—what life is all about. No false hopes here. Just the heat and air-conditioning.

I'm not you, Bill is chanting over and over again. At first you think he is sharing your opinion of the people on TV, but then it's clear he's referring to you. Gently, with something like pity in your voice, you tell him he's right. But he's not listening anymore.

Harvey has passed out on the bar, into the dice he has rolled—five 6s. The old people are staring at you as if it's your fault. Bill hasn't stopped his rambling. Though you can't remember having it filled again, your beer miraculously seems never to be empty. Donny flits along the bar like a ghost, filling empty glasses with his pale hands. Donny is one of those "taken for granted" things in life no one cares about. Just ask your wife.

You have a sudden vision that you are sitting across the bar; the thirteenth in the row of old men. You laugh nervously out loud—no one even notices your voice. Everyone is gone. If Jesus did appear here on a hot Sunday night, He would be sitting on the other side of the bar with you and the old men. Jesus would sit in the middle, talking of salvation and football. Then, oh then!—you'd exclaim that He's a union man, and a Bear's fan. That is when the quiet old men would hang Him above the jukebox on a Sunday night at the Rusty Nail.

Beholder

We were stranded in the desert and I pushed the sweat and hair from my eyes, trying to blink out the persistence of the sun. Gerry stood behind me, and I could hear his frustration through his breath. "Beautiful," the old man was saying, rocking back and forth in his chair. "The desert is beautiful. Don't you think?" The sand carried by a dry wind fell in the cracks on his porch, lazily bouncing across his worn boots. For a second the old man looked like an omen of vultures, then the hot air seemed to coalesce around his face, giving him an appearance of many possibilities. The house, porch, abandoned gas station, and the ragged old man looked out of place on the lonely stretch of highway.

I looked at Gerry. "Yes ma'am." The old man leaned closer to me. I could smell a spice in his breath—cinnamon? "Most men are blind and can't see beauty even if it's sitting on 'em." He winked a milky eye at me and glanced at Gerry, who was panting quietly. I turned to Gerry for him to say something, help me out. But he was lost in his anger at the car failing us, or his inability to understand the "why" of it stopping. It was hot, I had told him. But he wouldn't listen.

I turned back to the old man. His eyes looked as if he spent too much time considering the sun and its purpose. His hands were weaving private gestures over his knees like he was some kind of desert magician. The old man's face, like the desert, thirsted for water, and his hair had the aspect of sand falling downhill—it covered his dry face, almost burying the landscape beneath it.

"Sir, can we use your phone?" I asked him again. I had already explained to him that we were on our way to Las Vegas to be married, when our car broke down. I don't know why I told him where we were going. Maybe I thought the mention of our impending marriage would speed the car being repaired—draw a sympathy that could help. Or, maybe, it was his melancholic speech and dramatic face that pulled certain words from me.

"Sure." He locked those rheumy eyes on me, his face expressionless. Then he smiled, but that smile didn't alter his eyes as he said, "But . . . there's a price for the use of my phone."

"A price! C'mon Whitney, let's get out of here," Gerry blurted out unable to withstand the heat any longer.

Where? I wanted to say. We were a hundred miles from anywhere. The only thing we had seen was the "Oasis Gas 'Bout a 1/4 Mile Or So" sign that lead us here and marked the spot where our car broke down. It was as if the sign was an invisible boundary and the car wouldn't cross it. "Shh Gerry." I put my hand on his arm, trying to forestall another outburst, and turned back to the old man. "How much to use the phone?"

"'Bout a half hour or so." His voice, cracked words, stunned me, and for a moment I wondered if he, or I, was crazy—that the heat had fried our brains.

"Half hour?" I said. "What for? I mean, you don't want money?" Not that we had much. We had left with optimism and a thousand dollars we both had saved up from gradua-tion. We had four-hundred dollars and a hundred miles left for Vegas.

"No, no, deary. What do I need money for?" The old man gestured to his run-down gas station and the small shab-by house attached to it. The gas station looked as if it hadn't been used in years, and the house appeared better suited for ghosts.

"No, what I want is a bit of your time. Your ears." He finished with that small smile on his lips.

I looked at Gerry. His face was still flushed with heat even though evening was coming and the desert was cooling off. The hot wind died and Gerry echoed my question, "What for?"

"For? Why, for a chitchat." His smile widened, showing a few black spaces where teeth must have been at one time. "I'm here alone tonight." On the word "alone" a shadow seemed to fall over the house and gas station. Only the porch was illuminated by the setting sun.

"My wife is gone—I've no one to talk to . . . I think it would be a fair trade: you talk on my phone, I talk to you." All else was dark.

"I guess it'd be all right. Gerry?" I looked at him.

"Yeah. Go ahead. Why the hell not? We're not going anywhere." He plopped down in one of the two empty chairs occupying the porch. It was as if we, or any two travelers, were expected. Gerry sat back on the chair like an insolent child told to sit in the corner.

The old man gestured for me to sit in the other chair; I doubted it could hold my weight. He seemed to sense my hesitation. "Don't worry," he said, waving his hand as if he couldn't care less if I sat or not.

I sat gently onto the chair, surprised at the strength I felt in it. The old man nodded to himself, looking off into the desert, watching the sun set. Something in the way his eyes glinted from the waning sunlight made me want to hear what he had to say—made me want to know what this crazed old man was doing out here alone. This shabby house, run-down station, and the sun only shining on the porch demanded a story—and I would listen.

"What do you want to talk about?" I asked gently, wondering what it must be like to be alone and old. I wondered if my mother was lonely since my father died. I wondered if the old man's wife was dead, also, or had just gone off somewhere. I could feel Gerry fidgeting in his chair. I played with a strand of hair that had fallen into my eyes.

The old man leaned forward as if the closeness would reveal some secret from me—a secret we could somehow share together without Gerry. "I want to tell you a certain story. I like stories, don't you?" His voice stressed "certain," and the desert echoed it back. He twisted his head around to look at Gerry, as if it was up to him if we'd hear a story or not.

"Sure. Great. Can I have some milk and cookies too?" Gerry's sarcasm went by the old man because he nodded as if Gerry had given the proper response—the only.

"Tell," I said. "I'd love to hear a story." The words echoed in my head, and the house and gas station dissipated beneath and around me. He turned back to contemplate me. A pensive look disappeared into a warm smile. He locked eyes on me again. Somewhere in those depths was a sun—a brilliancy I couldn't define—a brilliancy suddenly desirable.

He settled back in his rocker, staring off again into the desert, waiting, I thought, for a signal. I watched his face and tried to figure out what he saw out there. Then, as if he was reading my thoughts, he tilted his head toward me as if he wanted to hear more. Abruptly, breaking the spell, he spoke.

"Beauty," he said, not looking at us. "Beauty is transitory. We never see it until it's gone."

"Desert philosophy. Shit, great," Gerry said from far away. The old man sighed. "Ah, my story. I forgot, you're in a hurry." He cleared his throat. "There was this boy, about twelve. He lived in a small town in Kansas with his parents and younger brother."

The creatures of the dark were starting their night songs in response to the old man's story. The desert movements and sounds held back all thoughts of road trips to Vegas, which fled with the day's heat.

"The boy could swim the whole length of the pond behind their house, underwater, without coming up for air. This impressed his younger brother to try it for himself. But something went wrong. The water wasn't deep, mind you, but I've heard of people drowning in bathtubs." The old man ran a hand across his leathery cheek as if bathtubs were something that should be considered, at least for a moment.

"The boy dove for his brother. And dove. He never thought of going for help because he judged it too far. He finally found him, but it was too late. His brother, it seems, had gotten tangled in the weeds at the bottom and panicked. His parents were heart struck. Though they didn't blame the boy for his brother's death, they were lost to themselves over the pain. As I said, a part of themselves was gone and they had nothing left to give the boy. You can't blame them—weren't they human, too?" The old man scratched his face and smiled.

The old man never took his eyes off the desert and the setting sun. Maybe, I thought, the desert itself was telling the story. I looked at Gerry who still seemed to be far away, and hoped he wouldn't say anything.

"Then, about a year went by since his brother drowned," the old man went on, oblivious to us. I wondered if he told this story to everyone who happened to stop by for help. "The boy never cried when he thought of his brother. By this time, his parents, remembering themselves, turned their attention to him—but it was too late."

He turned and again locked his eyes on me, and I wondered if he had been one of the parents. He turned back to the story.

"The boy seemed to have retreated into himself—he found a place where there were no tears—to survive. His parents were unaware of the change. His withdrawal. On the outside he looked the same. The boy didn't seem as happy as before, but it had only been a year since his brother died, the parents rationalized. The boy would go to school, then come home and go directly to his room, only emerging for supper to pick at his food."

I could feel Gerry getting closer, getting ready to speak. The old man seemed to feel it also, because he tilted his head toward Gerry, never taking his eyes off the desert. "Young man," the old man spat across the distance. "Have you no sympathy?" Then in a softer voice, "Have you no feelings?"

"Of course I do!" Gerry shot back.

"Sure you do," the old man mused. "Forgive me. Where was I? Oh yes, this boy went a whole year walking around in a kind of a daze. He had feelings he couldn't understand, much less explain."

My hands started to shake—I felt guilty. My thoughts seemed to be expanding with the night, and with the old man's story. The old man had stopped his narration, and was looking at me expectantly—as if I would corroborate his senseless story with my own, or maybe metamorphose into one of the desert's creatures. I wanted to scream at him to leave me out—to tell him I wasn't responsible for someone's loneliness, or a boy from Kansas; I wasn't running away from the plans my mother had for me. He turned back to the desert and the last of the sun.

"Everything looked pale to this boy, nothing held any color: the grass was gray, trees had turned to black shadows, and the sky became an empty palette. Even food held no taste for him, and games boys his age played held no interest, no meaning. They were like sand." He held out his arm and rubbed the tips of fingers together as if the memories were still present in his hand, refusing to let go to join their places with the wood-dust and sand of the porch.

"After a year of this the boy started staying up nights, unable to sleep. His mind raced and raced. He'd pace back and forth in his room, trying to catch his fleeing mind—but he couldn't. More and more he thought about his brother, and what it must be like to drown.

"Finally, one day, he couldn't take it. It was a Saturday and his parents had gone to visit some friends. He was outside in the backyard, pacing, trying to grasp his thoughts, when the meowing of a cat interrupted him. Instantly, as if on signal, everything became clear. He knew what he had to do to stop his mind."

The wind picked up speed in response to his story. The dry strands of the old man's hair swirled rhythmically around his face. It gave him the appearance of many different faces: a child's, an old man's, an Indian's, then a lion's. His voice turned aside the wind.

"The boy went into the house and found the small wire cage he and his brother used to catch rabbits. He enticed the cat into the cage with a bit of food. He latched the door and brought the cat into the house. He went into the bathroom and filled the tub with water.

"Frantic now, hurrying, the boy hoped to find the answer to his wandering mind. He brought the cage to the water. The cat, sensing the water, started to meow loudly, thrashing in the cage as if it knew his intent. The boy thrust the cage into the water, submerging it fully. He watched closely as the cat clawed at the empty spaces between the bars of the cage, looking for a way out to air."

The old man's hands were clenching and unclenching on his knees. His face was fire. The house and station were completely gone now—Gerry was gone. The porch, stage, only held me and the old man's different faces. The sun continued to set.

"The boy watched the cat closely—watched its eyes expectantly—looking for some answer in them. At the end, though, when he saw the cat's death reflecting from its eyes, something within the boy snapped. He pulled the cage out of the water, shaking it. The cat started spitting out water.

"While he was shaking the cage, the latch must've come undone. The cat shot out of the cage and onto the boy's face. It slashed once, then twice, then bounded away. Either by design, accident, or fate, the cat slashed both of the boy's eyes."

The sun was only a sliver of red across the old man's face, masking whatever pain his storytelling caused him. He began to hum a snatch of a song I couldn't quite recognize. Just as I thought I caught the tune, the old man continued.

"They took him to the hospital. The boy had enough sense left to go to the neighbor's house for help. Luckily, he wasn't blinded. The doctor told the boy that, eventually, it would be hard to see because the scar tissue would keep building up over time."

He looked at me with milky eyes.

"You," I whispered. "You're that boy."

His face was dark, the fading sunlight now was a cut across his chest. Tilting his head to include Gerry, he continued. "You see, that cat did me a favor. Ever since then, I have learned to see in different ways. Oh, not right away, or all at once to be sure, but I learned."

"Can we use the phone now?" Gerry asked.

You bastard, I thought. I wanted to scratch out his eyes. But the old man's face held me silent. I could see the scars the cat had left so many years ago. Or, maybe, I just wanted to see them.

"Sure sonny," the old man laughed. "But, just take the pail on the side, there," he pointed, "And fill it with water."

Gerry stared at him, not understanding.

"Now that the sun has gone down, your engine should be cooled enough to put water in the radiator—seen it ha pen a million times. You know what a radiator is?"

"Yeah, I know. I'm not stupid." Gerry stood and went for the pail.

"Are you blind?" I asked.

He shook his head to the side.

I could hear the faucet pouring out water on the side of the house. "Are you here alone?" I hurried.

Again, he shook his head.

"C'mon, Whitney! Let's go," Gerry called from the road, sloshing the water in the pail.

"Do you . . . I mean . . . " I hesitated, then I said in a rush. "Did you hate that cat—for what it did?"

"No. I found him again, later. We became good friends."

"Whitney!" Gerry had already started down the road without me. The old man rose from his chair and started to shuffle for the darkness of his house as if to beat the curtain of night that was falling.

"Keep it," he said, anticipating my next question. "Unless you continue down the road to Vegas—then you can drop it off." He saw the confusion in my face. "Don't you know where you're going?" He pointed in the opposite direction Gerry was taking, toward Las Vegas. I grabbed his hand and squeezed, then ran to catch up with Gerry, and the pail.

A Memoir of the Unique Man

I.

I didn't actually try to kill myself. I mean, sure, it could've looked that way, but my heart wasn't in it—if you know what I mean. But I'll get to that later—it's not important right now. Now Jonathan, my friend, his heart was in it.

Jonathan called, the day before. I was so sick that I couldn't—wouldn't talk to him. Jonathan, you see, was an alcoholic; breakfast for him was a liter of cheap vodka.

I was in the hospital that Monday, the day he did it, a habit that I would become familiar with for the next three years. I was sick. I had a fire in my bones that wouldn't go out. The doctors called it osteomyelitis; I called it "the fire that almost took my life."

Anyway, I was lying there in my antiseptic, drab room, wondering why all hospital rooms look and smell the same. Hell, they could've moved me at night and I never would've known the difference. The call from Jonathan came that afternoon, at least I think it did.

"Steven?" a voice said.

"Yes." I was flying a Demerol plane—blotto.

"Jonathan's dead. He put a .22 to his head, right between the eyes. He even bothered to take off his glasses to accommodate the blackness. The bullet didn't even exit." The voice mused in a dead litany.

"And by the by, he left a little note for you. It said, 'Tell Steven I just gave up. He'll understand.' Do you?" the voice demanded.

"Of course," I shot back in a heroic effort to land my high.

"Of course," came the reply, then the phone went dead. *Buzz.*

Later, I came to, holding a whining receiver in my hand. Was I calling someone? Did someone call me? Apparently not, so I hung it up and went off into space again. It wasn't until later that I realized that I hadn't been dreaming.

That day, I had emergency surgery to stop the infection they said I had from reaching out and touching my heart. I was so far gone. It wasn't until a week later that I realized that I actually had a name. My eyes felt as if somebody had pissed on them—I had a hard time focusing on my wife, who had materialized next to my bed. "How do you feel, Steve?" she whispered, as if my ears were the things that hurt.

"Like someone pissed on my face." I bravely smiled to show her that I was the man that she married. "Give me some nails, honey."

"What?" She didn't get the joke, her face screwed up into a fist of pity.

"A joke," I rasped. "Water."

She held a straw to my mouth and I sipped away greedily, sloughing away the nasty film in my mouth. They must've pissed there, too.

"Don't try to talk. The doctor says you'll be weak for a few more days yet. You've been out for almost a week."

"A week?" I said, every word I spoke was making me dizzy. "Why so long?"

"The doctor says the pain was so intense that they had to keep you sedated. When you came out of recovery . . . you were screaming at the nurses—pulling out your tubes from your arms." I could see she was holding back a trembling lip.

I gave her my best "I'm-a-man" smile. "I'm better now."

Whatever they were giving me was wearing off, and an intense pain was traveling from my right leg to my foggy brain. A nurse came in carrying a syringe.

"Time for your pain medication, Mr. Gonzales." She seemed eager to give it to me, and I was needing it, so . . . who was I to argue? She pulled up the flimsy gown and pressed it into me. As the drug fought its way to my heart, I felt myself filling up with clouds. Aha! now I knew where the piss feeling came from.

"Casey," I slurred—the drug overtaking me. I hurried. "You know I had the weirdest dream, right before they took me in. I dreamt," I was talking slower and slower, "that someone called me and told me Jonathan killed himself."

Unable to hold back, she let the tears roll down her face. "Rest, Steven."

I did.

I was standing in what we called the *swamp*—his room. Jonathan was sitting on his bed, a full bottle of vodka next to him. "Here." He pointed to the bottle, "I'm not even drunk."

I couldn't speak, this was his time. He shook his head back and forth, as if the mere movement meant something I should understand. He picked up a black broom and put the handle between his eyes. "You know, a man is nobody without a job."

I wanted to scream at him to put the broom down.

He looked at me as if he heard my thoughts. "No Steve, it's time to sweep out the cobwebs." The broom handle exploded and I then got the scream out.

The nurse poked me in the arm again, and I was gone.

I tried to call Jonathan's brother to give my regrets, but he hung up on me. Well, I was hurt. So, I figured as far as I was concerned they could all burn, including Jonathan.

I no longer had, nor wanted, any more friends.

II.

After two years of being in and out of the hospital, I was starting to believe the doctors—that there was nothing more wrong with me. But why did I still burn? I had thirty surgeries in all by this time. Somehow Casey and I managed to have two children: a boy and a girl. We were lucky because the paper mill's insurance covered both births. But that was it: no more sick benefits, no more health insurance (for my wife and kids) and finally, no more job. One benefit from being home sick was that I got to spend more time with the kids. But, again, that wouldn't last either.

We were broke. We borrowed from her father. We borrowed from my father. Then I sold my toys: camper, motorcycle (I loved that bike), all my guns—everything we could do without. I was also, by this time, addicted to Percodan. I had pain.

I went six whole weeks without a surgery, and the doctors said things were looking up. Then one day, the fire went out of control and even the pain pills weren't working. I went back to my doctor and he said he couldn't find anything wrong with me. Maybe, he rationalized, you're addicted to pain medication. And maybe it was all in my mind—and, maybe, he didn't want to see me any more.

My insurance company must've felt the same way because they sent me to Milwaukee to see a specialist in disease control. Now, I was not only sick, but I had to leave my home and drive two hundred miles south to Milwaukee; this would be my first time ever there. I reluctantly agreed to go: my wife reluctantly agreed; my family reluctantly agreed. We were on welfare when I left my home, and my family.

III.

In Milwaukee, at the hospital, they found not only was the pain in my head, but because of the multiple surgeries, I now had pain and the disease throughout my body. I was dying for the second time. I decided to stay in Milwaukee for treatment.

My wife couldn't make the trip—a three and some odd hour drive—and besides, she had my babies to take care of. I was alone.

I was getting a combination chemotherapy and immunotherapy. I could throw up in Technicolor. I went from 210 to 150 pounds in just a couple weeks—amazing diet plan.

My wife promised she would come to see me soon. The phone bills were getting out of hand, she said. Maybe we should only talk once a week.

My doctors were creating fantastic combinations of drugs to kill the pain—pain was my one foe, now. My body was so immune to the medications that nothing I was given would kill the pain. But God bless them, they tried to keep up with my changing metabolism.

I was also dreaming more and more of Jonathan. I'd see him sitting at my bedside with his legs crossed. He would just sit there and look at me with that silly hole between his eyes. I never spoke to him. We had a mutual agreement: don't speak to me, and I won't speak to you.

My parents started to come to visit me, reluctantly. I could see the shame in their eyes for not really believing that I was sick. There was no question by then: I looked like a bag of bones with pink skin. Chemo does that to you. But hey, I had my hair.

They'd tell me about my kids, and show me pictures to prove that they were still mine. Too traumatic for them to see their dad this way, they said. Of course, I'd smile. They flinched—my teeth had turned black. My wife would come next time, they promised—then waved good-bye. They had been there a whole hour.

The time I tried to kill myself is hilarious. You see, I disconnected the tubes, IV tubes, from my chest. They had two tubes going directly to my heart, because the fluid going in was just too caustic for the regular little veins. I popped those suckers off and watched the blood spurt all over my sheets. Jonathan was sitting in the chair, as usual, and was laughing without sound.

I thought he was happy that I had decided to join him. But later, I figured he was laughing because he knew that hospitals take all sorts of precautions, like the catheters have safety valves in case they pop off. I never told anyone that I did it—I was just so embarrassed. I had been there for six months and I was beginning to believe that I would never die.

My wife came to see me the sixth month I was in Milwaukee. She put up a brave front, but I could tell she was uncomfortable with me and my black smile. The bills were getting out of control, she said. What was she to do? She was thinking of getting a job. She was tired of using food stamps.

A job would do her good, I told her. I smiled. She turned away. I told her the doctors said that I was recovering. We were winning. They said maybe I could leave the hospital for an afternoon. What did she think of that?

She didn't believe me or my doctors anymore. She was nothing, she said—nothing but somebody who would wait to hear that her husband was dead. She was empty, she said. I looked over at Jonathan; he didn't even acknowledge me.

I did form a few friendships with the other cancer patients—but they weren't long ones, if you know what I mean. I made friends with some of the families that visited our ward. I did get to go out the seventh month with a friend I had made at the hospital. It was my first time being outside in Milwaukee.

I recovered. My disease went into remission. I told my wife, and she asked when I was coming home. Soon, I told her, and then I could maybe go back to work!

That was the end of the seventh month; I weighed 151 pounds. You could've killed an elephant with the amount of pain medication I was taking, the nurses told me.

The doctor said I was addicted to drugs, and that I needed what he termed, "post-traumatic therapy." I was to spend three more months in a mental hospital for drug therapy, which coincidentally, was how long my insurance would last.

My wife couldn't believe what I was doing to her life and told me if I wasn't home in a month, she wasn't going to be there for me. Oh, well.

IV.

Jonathan didn't follow me to the psych ward; I don't think he wanted therapy that far into his death.

I came to terms with my drug problem. Well, they did anyway. I had no choice . . . and no drugs. When Jonathan went away, I realized how much I missed him. A funny thing, that fall from the MPD Airways (I call it the Morpho-Perco-Demerol Airways) when you hit the tarmac, there is no grass to save your ass. You find there is nothing there to break your fall: no friends, no family. The friends you have are the other passengers on the same flight.

My brother called me one day—I was about 158 pounds at that time, I think. He told me that he'd seen an old friend's truck parked in my driveway for a whole evening. He was sure. Back then I was measuring time in pounds—I was someone who was just passing time and taking up air on earth. I no longer had a wife.

I divorced my wife. I didn't have the heart to tell her that I knew she was having an affair. I figured I put her through enough. I lied and told her that I'd met someone in the hospital who cared for me—and she wasn't needed. I hadn't seen my kids in a whole year. My parents were appalled. My brother probably knew the truth, but he never said.

I gained more weight, and it seemed my brains were gaining weight. I was starting to remember things I had forgotten for the last three years. I remembered our wedding day when Casey said "I do." I remembered the feeling of completeness when she told me she was pregnant the first time.

Jonathan was sitting on his bed, holding a gun between his eyes. "You're a goddamn nobody," I screamed at him. "Where were you when I needed you?" He smiled at that, and his teeth were rotten. He pulled the trigger and blackness burned around the barrel. His head shook from side to side. The bullet never came out, a voice said—a narrator. His head swayed in a tremendous wind, his eyes never leaving mine. His lips formed words, "You're a nobody. A man without family is not a man. Where were *you?*"

V.

The lady from vocational rehab says that technical school is a good choice for me. She even helped me find an apartment here in Milwaukee.

With what I get from Social Security, I should be able to live comfortably. Even my kids get money—neat, huh? I can walk with hardly any pain at all. I haven't taken so much as an aspirin in the last two weeks. My dad called the other day to tell me that, eventually, they will forgive me if I'll make up with my wife—excuse me, ex-. I'll try, I told him. I lied.

My disease will always be there, my doctor said. Anytime, a week, a year—ten . . . anytime, I could be back to where I was. But I don't worry too much about it.

I take walks around my neighborhood, trying to become familiar with the area. I don't have many friends. The ones I do have are still in the psych ward—I don't keep track of the cancer patients. I weigh about 170 pounds now, and sometimes I get to see my kids. It's hard for them to remember me. I take the bus up north or my brother brings them to Milwaukee—well, once. Call me "Uncle," I told them. I don't think I'll see them much anymore.

My brother still calls once in a while, but not as much as he used to.

School is interesting. For now, I take basic courses. I haven't been in school for a long time—I'm what . . . three years . . . ah yes, twenty-nine. I don't have any set goals at this time. Late at night, when I can't sleep and start to think about flying the MPD Airways again, I'll walk around my neighborhood—I'm not afraid.

The other night I stopped in the Fifth District Police Department. I was curious, so I just limped on in, surprised the hell out of the woman seated at the front desk. I went over to the bulletin board and started to browse the pamphlets. The policewoman asked if I needed help. I told her I was just looking. She nodded, but still kept an eye on me. "Neighborhood Watch Program," one pamphlet said. "Take a Bite Out of Crime," was another.

I noticed on the wall there were pictures of policemen. I went and scanned over them. They were men who had died in the line of duty. Each plaque had on it: "So-and-So Died in the Line of Duty."

I was fascinated by the faces of these men, who all died for something. They seemed so real to me. One plaque, I think it was the oldest on the wall, had an additional inscription that the others didn't have. It said in faded letters: "There are a hundred-thousand like Him, but we came to know Him. *Now*, He is unique to the world." That made me smile.

Mousetrap

1.

I stand in front of the full-length mirror in the room that my parents shared, and in that reflection, at my shoulder, stands my newly-dead father. At his shoulder stands his father. I am the one who is not smiling. My mother is white and French, and cries alone for my father, elsewhere. My father's belongings, neatly piled as if readied for a long trip, are the background of this picture of us three. My grandfather's letters to my father crest the pile, waiting for me to see. Now, my legacy. If I want them or not. An ambiguous start.

2.

She wants you to come to Paris, my first home, my mother was saying. She called, waking me to tell me my father was dead. In his sleep. Always it happens in the sleep. Same as your grandfather. Your grandmother is ready to forgive "us," my mother said. Really me. My mother was white and not Chinese as she was supposed to be. An accident of birth, and love. My mother was trying not to cry, don't come home to Paris. Stay in Chicago where you are safe from *her*. Don't come. I left that afternoon—flew back across an incredible gulf of loneliness.

3.

In this story is the story of my father's making; how he defied his mother and married beyond the bounds of propriety; how he fell in love with a white woman and not the Chinese woman that was chosen for him. This is the story of how my father broke his mother's heart. This is of my father's heart breaking. My grandfather stood by silently and watched it all unfold. It starts with mice.

4.

My father assigned the job of keeping the mice out of our apartment to me. I would plant the traps around the house in corners, using peanut butter as bait. For every one you see, my father told me, there are ten more. I saw three mice. I remember lying awake at night dreading the sound of the traps as they snapped shut. This is how stories are; they are traps waiting to snap shut—to capture you inside.

5.

My grandfather's letters were neatly piled, in order of time. Some speak of Vietnam, before it fell to the communists. Others are postmarked from across town, Paris. From another planet. My grandmother forebade him to see my father, his son. A joke played upon him by my great-grandfather, who doesn't share my reflections. My great-grandfather had given control of all the money to my grandmother when he died. A joke. This is all told through the letters that lie poised to ensnare me into Grandfather's story. A bait I cannot refuse: a joke. I was the only one allowed to see Grandfather.

6.

I knew the letters were there for me to decipher. My mother had left them there, and I decided time was too precarious. I started to read them from the middle. Skimming time on my tiptoes on a high wire. There were funerals to attend. My father's and mine. My grandmother spat at the ground. At my mother's feet, with an eloquence that defied sorrow or words. I was tempted to cry. I was only half Chinese anyway.

7.

On top of each letter, in my father's hand, is written: **Father writes**. It drips of sarcasm and love.

The Mekong River is sluggish, before the rains, and dark as the thick French coffee I sipped in my Paris cafés. The heat pulls my breath from me and I wonder how I'll ever draw another. The ferry crossing is made bearable by the sight of the young white girl. She is wearing a man's hat. That is how she is distinguishable from the world around her. She looks no older than fifteen. She is leaning against the railing, forever in my memory, watching the Mekong flow. She seems to be enjoying the role the river is playing in my falling in love with her. I don't even know her name.

The letters are old. Some are more brown than others. My friends back in Chicago used to remark at my skin color, trying to place me in their world. My name. My family. But names are not important. Only places and things have names: the Mekong, Paris, Vietnam, and mice. People exist among them and disappear into reflections that tell stories of the past. I am only my father's son, and he is his father's son. My mother tells me I should leave Paris and go back to Chicago—to school—not stating the obvious. It is never obvious in stories. My grandmother wants me. The letters tell me that. Yet, how can I tell my mother I have no choice but to stay and marry into my grandmother's dream? The choice that was determined on a ferry crossing the Mekong; a choice my father has finally fulfilled in his and my death— my death because I died years ago in my grandfather's reflection. Instead, I'll tell my mother she cannot survive on the stories. The letters are mine, now.

8.

Mice are in stories. When I woke in the morning, I checked the mousetraps. My father said he would pay me a franc for every ten I caught. I had lined up four traps against the wall—all in a row. I caught four mice; each walked over their dead family to get to the bait and trap . . . and so on. I remember crying as I disposed of them. I needed six more for a franc. And if what my father said was true, there were forty more mice left. Words are bait.

9.

The letters tell me the story that is not there—how my grandfather defied his own father and loved a young French girl while in Vietnam. Some of the letters are just journal entries sold to my father as an excuse. My grandfather defied his father's story and placed himself in the trap—he became a mouse, and lost. He was forced by his fear of poverty to abandon the white girl and marry the one that was chosen for him: my grandmother. As final punishment, his father gave all the control to her. I know my grandmother loves me as only the Chinese can.

10.

I am six and my father passes my hand to my grandfather in the park. I can feel their affection transferred through me. I love you, my father says to me. Me too, my grandfather smiles at me. I am alone with each of them.

11.

My mother has used up all her tears, and sleeps.

12.

The heat of her skin as she touched me, there, had left a burning only penetration could satisfy. She told me, in my limo, when I was taking her where she wanted to go, that she was eighteen. A lie. I am thirty, I told her. Oh, she said, not surprised or worried. I knew she was younger—younger than what my father could keep me out of prison for. This only made me burn hotter for her. She slept in the afternoon heat and I traced a finger over her breasts, knowing I was, then, in love with her—yet, she didn't love me. She awoke and the fire exploded as I did. Inside of her, again. And again. A thirst that would not quiet. I knew her name. She was the one I could never love.

In his letters, my grandfather baited my father, but the story is incomplete. Histories are also traps. The reader searches for the meaning in the bait, examining the words as if they are true—have meaning. This is the mousetrap. In *this* story, I will touch other stories: my story, my father's story, his father's story, but not his father's. And I will talk to Gerald Vizenor, a Native American writer. He says, "Stories are interior landscapes." His is the only name I will use—the rest have no names. We and they are mice scurrying among the pages. This is now the story of four generations—and Gerald Vizenor.

13.

I didn't do it against my mother, going to my grand-mother to hear her words. I let her hold me as she cried for my father, and her son. The tears were angry on my cheek. She didn't tell me I looked like my father when he was my age. She only cried and said I had been away too long. In that place. She could not say America. It was the hate for my mother sending me there. My mother's only defiance of her—besides marrying my father.

14.

If you marry her, I will not be able to stop your mother from excising you from the family, and money. I do not have any control she does not give. Remember who you are? This is the last time she will allow me to communicate with you if you keep up this charade. I don't have the strength to defy her. Your mother wants you to marry the girl she has picked out.

15.

My memories would be different in my grandmother's dreams. My existence among mice evading the stories. Gerald says, "Survival is imagination, a verbal noun, a wild transitive word in my mixedblood autobiographies; genealo-gies, the measured lines in our time, and place, are never the same in personal memories. Remembrance is a natural cur-rent that beats and breaks with the spring tides; the curious imagine a sensual undine on the wash, as the nasturtiums dress the barbed wire fences down to the wild sea."

The Mekong swells to almost a third its size during the rainy season. My heart is the Mekong. My father has threatened to send me back to Paris to finish business school. He has threatened because he would make me poor. The Khone Falls on the border of Cambodia, I am told, run as the devil. It is a sight to behold— I am told. I still love her.

16.

My father awoke early in the mornings. He fixed break-fast for my mother and me. Croissants and coffee. My mother was taking photography classes at my high school. We left in the mornings together—my father cleaned up after us. We left my father there, alone, in the mornings. Everyday.

17.

I knew, through his letters, that my grandfather had this need to tell my father about his affair with a fifteen-year-old white girl, as if this would make all that has happened between them disappear. Into letters. There was no compar-ison between them as there was no comparison between the pictures of me with my grandparents, and those of me with my mother and father. Tradition, with my grandmother starched behind me, a hand on my shoulder. Don't smile, look knowledgeable, she whispered in my ear. In my other pictures, we are all smiling. I know then, as we laugh and pose together. In those nontraditional poses I realize I will always love my grandmother. Still, I will never understand. I will always be in the seams of these contrasts.

18.

Gerald Vizenor is a trickster. "Famous writers spend too much time alone with their style, carving their experiences with the past," says the trickster. "No one has ever come alive in blank verse, or as an objective complement," he says and leaps to the rafters. He poises there with one eye closed. "Love and passion are never left to dull men who create his-tories from their collection of tame words, or from grammars. Some people put things together, and others take things apart, but tricksters and little people float between words and dreams. Maybe that was seams." Gerald is a visionary.

19.

I was forced to give her up, even though I don't think she loved me. Not only because it was expected, but because I had no choice. Your mother does not have any forgiveness for you. When your son gets older I will send him wherever he wants to go. I will provide for him what I can—that much she will allow. He is family.

20.

The letters are all the same. The same guilt-enfolded pages. I can see the impressions where the money lay. The folding of them tells much more than the words inside. Silence. Years and years, they and I knew. I always knew that my mother was not welcomed there. We never spoke of it here, or there. The trickster in the rafters winks and laughs at our poses.

21.

In the morning, the phone rings. I am fifteen, like his white girl. There is silence on the receiver. It is for me. That is how my grandmother and I communicate. When my mother or father answers, she tells them with her imposed silence who the call is for; for you, my mother says, unconcerned by the woman on the other end. Grandmother, I tell her in Chinese though she speaks perfect French—she upholds tradition on the telephone. Your grandfather is dead. In his sleep. Tell your father, this is the one time she and I will speak of my father, and the last until my father dies. Me, fifteen, like a white girl, I go to my father as in those traditional poses, knowledgeable. He is dead. Your father. My grandfather. My father is a man who is not afraid to cry.

22.

In the rafters the trickster laughs and twists his ear, and I am walking behind my father in traditional dreams, holding his hand. I am fifteen and my grandmother walks ahead of us, leading the silent procession to place my grandfather away, forever. The mausoleum is new green marble, with the symbol of the dragon above the door. My hand sweats in my father's, and with the other hand I tug at the mole behind my ear. I share reflections with the trickster. I can see the Eiffel Tower in the distance. My father lets go of my hand— he can go no further. He is not allowed. My grandmother turns and sees my father in his place, and smiles. I pull at the mole on my ear and I am in the rafters. The trickster is compassionate.

23.

The three of us meet on the Eiffel Tower, secretive as spies. I can see they are happy to be so high.

24.

When a mouse is caught by its tail it will drag the trap to the hole it would escape into. But it can't because the trap holds the tail fast, and will not fit into the hole. The reader of stories is caught by the words and the escape to reality is denied. In the end, like with the mouse, it doesn't matter. Reality is just a hole.

I found the mouse the next morning, struggling weakly to enter its sanctuary. Over and over, I thought, this mouse stubbornly tried to escape. And the night was long. In my ten-year-old mind I couldn't fathom *forever*. It was a dark tunnel that tried to suck my thoughts away into shadows. I cried as I struck the mouse with a large silver spoon—over and over. Forever is a long time and that mouse would still be there today, trying to escape with its tail caught in a trap.

25.

I have never been to Vietnam, the former colony of my grandmother's people. The letters talk of it as a wonderfully hot place. The Mekong is in my dreams now. I will marry into a powerful family, my grandmother tells me. All that is asked of me. Nothing more. The letters become unimportant as I read through them. The same. I knew this all before. The words wander as a slow dark river, going nowhere.

26.

One letter has been ripped up and taped whole. I will not read one that tears up history and then tries to mend it. The envelope has no address, only the word "please?" on the front. A question. There is no postmark—no destination. Just a question of propriety. There is dark humor in a mouse caught with its tail in a trap; a mouse who would do better to chew its own appendage off to escape into a hole.

27.

My mother and I will not speak of my impending marriage, ever. It is part of the agreement that we will make, together.

28.

This is not a story.

Acknowledgments and Thanks

Kimberly Blaeser is a professor of English at the University of Wisconsin–Milwaukee and a member and one of the founders of the writing group Word Warriors. She has two books recently published, *Trailing You*, 1994, a collection of poetry from Greenfield Review Press, and a critical study entitled, *Gerald Vizenor: Writing in the Oral Tradition*, 1996, University of Oklahoma Press.

Amy E. De Jarlais is a writer extraordinaire and a member of Word Warriors in Milwaukee, Wisconsin, where she is a student.

Ralph Grajeda is the director of Latino and Latin American Studies at the University of Nebraska–Lincoln.

Jim Gutierrez and **Jose Berrios** are both song writers and musicians from Chicago, Illinois, who will soon be releasing their first CD.

Stellia Jordán Orozco is a native of Cali, Colombia, who now lives in Milwaukee with her seven-year-old daughter, Adriana. Stellia has her master's in foreign language and literature, and currently teaches Spanish at the University of Wisconsin–Milwaukee.

Peter Whalen is a poet and teacher from Milwaukee, working on his Ph.D. in creative writing at the University of Wisconsin–Milwaukee, and also is a member of Word Warriors. His works include an audio presentation of his poetry on cassette entitled *The Mayan Way*.

About the Author

The second of five children, Lupe Solis, Jr. was born in Neenah, Wisconsin, in 1960. His father is Chicano and his mother is Polish American. He has three children: Justin, Stefan, and Whitney. He has served in the army, and he has been a mill worker and an insurance salesman. He is finishing his Ph.D. in creative writing at the University of Wisconsin–Milwaukee, where he teaches minority literature and creative writing, and where he is a member of Word Warriors, a multicultural writers' group.